George Carter Stent

Entombed Alive and Other Songs, Ballads &c.

George Carter Stent

Entombed Alive and Other Songs, Ballads &c.

ISBN/EAN: 9783744787123

Printed in Europe, USA, Canada, Australia, Japan

Cover: Foto ©Andreas Hilbeck / pixelio.de

More available books at **www.hansebooks.com**

AND

OTHER SONGS, BALLADS, &c.

(FROM THE CHINESE.)

BY

GEORGE CARTER STENT, M.R.A.S.,

OF THE CHINESE IMPERIAL MARITIME CUSTOMS SERVICE.

AUTHOR OF "CHINESE AND ENGLISH VOCABULARY,"
"CHINESE AND ENGLISH POCKET DICTIONARY," "THE JADE CHAPLET,"
ETC.

LONDON:

WILLIAM H. ALLEN AND CO.,

13 WATERLOO PLACE, PALL MALL, S.W.

———

1878.

TO

ROBERT HART, Esq.,

INSPECTOR GENERAL OF H. I. C. M. CUSTOMS,

WHO IS EVER READY TO ASSIST BY HIS COUNTENANCE

AND SUPPORT ANY WORK

TENDING TO INCREASE AN INTEREST IN,

AND KNOWLEDGE OF, CHINA AND THE CHINESE,

THIS VOLUME

IS RESPECTFULLY DEDICATED BY HIS

OBEDIENT SERVANT,

THE AUTHOR.

PREFACE.

ing assured, whatever its faults may be, the perusal will afford *some* amusement, and also disclose many curious customs of a country comparatively unknown to the general English reader.

G. C. S.

4th December 1878.

CONTENTS.

ENTOMBED ALIVE.

Oh, what a fearful dream! Thank God I woke!
  I thought I was within a noisome tomb immured,
Where all was dark; no sound the silence broke—
  Ah, who can tell the terrors I endured!

Too horror-struck to even form a prayer,
  I could but writhe upon the ground and scream;
Curse my hard fate, give way to wild despair,
  And, wake at length—to find it all a dream.

I'll call my maid and bid her strike a light,
  For even now I feel oppressed with fear;
How cold I am—I'll sleep no more to night;
  I shall feel better when the girl is here.

1

She does not come! Wherefore this awful gloom?
  Why does my heart thus beat with unknown dread?
How came I hither? This is not my room,
  It seems but little larger than my bed.

This is not my couch—'tis clammy ground!
  Above my head a roof of stone I feel—
Stone, too, on either side—stone all around!
  It *is* a tomb! Great God! my dream is *real!*

Help! Save me! Let me not die like this—
  A living death! Will no one heed my cries?
I stagger up, and reach an orifice,
  To which I glue my hot and blood-shot eyes.

I never knew how beautiful it was till now,
  To watch the rising sun his radiance throw
O'er hill and dale, on every bush and bough—
  Tinging all nature with a golden glow.

Help! Hither! Save me! Come and set me free!
  My piercing screams attract the passers by;—
Oh! are you men? Can you look on and see
  A girl—a woman—shut up thus to die?

'Tis not the dread of death my heart appalls;
  It is this lingering, living death I fear,—
Shut up alive, to die within these walls,
  Where every moment lengthens to a year.

Break down these walls! What if my crime was great,
  Say, could it merit such a death as this!
Kill me at once—if death *must* be my fate—
  The hand that strikes the welcome blow, I'll kiss!

Help, I implore you! 'Tis a woman calls!
  I'm young and fair! Oh, save me from this death!
Oh, snatch me from this tomb, break down these walls—
  And I will bless you with my latest breath!

Help! Give me but my liberty—my life!
  Save me from death—from this my living grave!
Whoever saves me, I will be his wife—
  His mistress—leman—minion—menial—slave!

Poor though he be, his poverty I'll share;
  The whole devotion of a life I'll give!
I'll toil for him—his troubles I will bear—
  I'll beg for him—so he but bids me live!

Help! I am stifling! Oh! for the fresh pure air!—
  To feel it on my hot and fevered cheeks!
Help! Save me! or my very hands shall tear
  These cursed walls! I'll rend them with my shrieks!

Water! One drop, to quench my maddening thirst!
  My tongue is swollen—my throat is parched and dry!
Can this be death?—Father, you've done your worst,
  But oh! 'twas hard to doom me thus to die!

1 *

The circumstances on which the foregoing verses are founded took place at Pekin about twenty-five years ago. The facts were these:—*Chun-tu-lao-yeh,* 春都老爺, a well-known censor, who lived near the Tung-ssu-pai-lou, 東四牌樓, had a daughter, aged twenty-one, who fell in love with one of the servants, a carter, and eventually eloped with him. They were captured by the patrol, when some distance from Peking, and brought back prisoners. The father caused the man to be banished, and had his daughter *built in a tomb* in the family cemetery, where she was left to die.

The cemetery where she was entombed alive is distant from Peking about twenty *li,* in a southerly direction from the Tung-chih-mên 東直門. The tomb was built of brick and plastered over with mud, with a small square hole in front of it, so that she was visible to those who wished to see her. The cemetery was open, having no walls round it, but having a man to look after it. Numbers of persons visited the tomb out of curiosity, and saw the girl through the hole, but no one attempted to rescue her, although entreated to do so by her in the most heart-rending language.

My informant both saw and heard the girl himself, and he describes her entreaties and cries of despair as awful in the extreme. She died on the fourth day of her incarceration, some say from poison, administered in water, which she drank ravenously, as her continual screaming must have parched her throat. Many of the lookers on entreated the man in charge to save her, but he dared not do it, for fear of the consequences to himself.

That such horrible barbarity is by no means extinct among the Chinese will be obvious to all who have read or will read the description in the *North-China Daily News* of the 20th May 1874, of a son having been buried alive for the murder of his father.

The author of the following verses supposes the victim to awake during the darkness of the night, in her living tomb, from a fearful dream that she has been buried alive. At first her sense of relief is intense at finding that she has only been dreaming. But by-and-bye she realises that she is indeed entombed, and, as day dawns, she is able to see through the hole the people passing by. These she attracts by her shrieks, and tries to influence by her pathetic appeals; but in vain! Delirium and death darkly close the scene.

THE FLIGHT OF HSIEN-FENG *
TO JEHOL.†

When the English and French first went up to Peking—
This was in the tenth year of the reign of *Hsien fêng*—
The news flew like wildfire, the tocsin was rung ; ‡
What a hubbub the whole of the city was in !

---

* The above poem is remarkable, as a specimen of native political satire reminding one in its coarser parts of some passages in Peter Pindar (Dr. Wolcott). It was, obviously, written by one of the officials who accompanied the Emperor Hsien-fêng in his flight from the Allies' attack on Peking in 1860. On its publication it was at once put on the *Index Expurgatorius* at Peking, and its publication and sale can now be effected only in a clandestine manner.

† A summer residence of the Emperors of China, named after a stream which flows near, called by foreigners Jehol, the characters being 熱 河 Je-ho, " Warm Stream."

‡ The Emperor was staying in the Summer Palace when the Allied Forces were on their way to Peking. As they

Pell-mell, off the Ministers instantly ran
To the palace, to ascertain what could be done ;
They all, with one voice, begged their sovereign to run—
Or rather *retire*—for a time to Mu-lan.*

———

    'Twas in the eighth moon,
    On the eighth day, at noon,—
Or it ought to have been,—but they started too soon.†
    The Imperial cart ‡
    Was ready to start,
And off went *Hsien-fêng* with a pit-a-pat heart §

———

advanced, the news was rapidly conveyed to Peking by
couriers, relays of horses and men being placed at short
stages on the road. From Peking to the "Summer
Palace" dismounted men were posted within hail of each
other the entire distance, so that the news of the advance
of the troops was passed from one to the other, *vivâ voce*,
in an incredibly short space of time.

  * Another name for Jehol.

  † The order was given to start at noon, but, so great
was the eagerness to be off, that they started at break of
day.

  ‡ Cart, is the term used here, and at several other
places. The Emperor used a sedan-chair.

  § *Chia-ching*, the grandfather of *Hsien-fêng*, died at
Jehol ; this was considered a very unfortunate circumstance, as *dying away from home*. On that account Tao-
kuang, his son, never once during his reign went there,
and *Hsien-fêng* dreaded going there, but was compelled by
circumstances to do so. The wealthy inhabitants had
already left Peking, flying in all directions.

His followers and escort,
And people of that sort,
Were really in quite a deplorable state;
A more wretched plight
Never broke on the sight,—
For at sixes and sevens were the guards of the gate.

Isn't it strange?
A miraculous change
Has come over these swells;—can they be the same men
Who would swagger and fuss,
Look down so on us?
What a wonderful difference betwixt now and then!

Their pride's had a fall,
And they look rather small;
The face of each worthy's a picture of woe;
Not one is prepared,
They well may look scared,
For, ready or not, they've the order to go.

It comes pretty hard
On the Emperor's guard
No matter at all in what light you may put it;
Those who hav'n't a nag,
Must their weary legs drag
All the way to Jehol—for they've all got to foot it.

The guards from the Banners *now* look no great shakes,
For so sudden a flight a great difference makes;

And the same men who formerly turned out so spruce,
Look as if all their smartness had gone to the deuce.

No two were alike—some came out in gauze—
Right or wrong they apparently cared not two straws ;
Here, one fellow sported his tassels and tags,
His " next man," perhaps, being almost in rags.

One a summer hat wore, one, a hat made of felt—
Though the heat was sufficient to make a man melt :
There were trousers and leggings of various hues,—
Some sported their boots, some their sandals or shoes ;

Some wore their long coats and some wore their short,
Of this shape and fashion, of that kind and sort ;
This wore a swell robe, that a short hunter's skirt—
But every one wore—a good thick coat of dirt.

Of the spears which displayed the well known leopard's
        tail,
Half were carelessly carried or dropped to the trail ;*
We had no heart to keep up appearances now,
And we went on pell-mell—as we liked—any how.

---

    * These guards ought always, when on duty with the
Emperor to have their spears at the " carry ; " they were
evidently " riding at ease."

On we marched, the hot sun peeled the skin off the
    nose;
The blisters came out on our soles, heels, and toes;
Those who tramped it were soon so entirely fagged
    out,
That the calves of their legs and their shins changed
    about.

Tired, hungry and thirsty, still on we all marched—
My throat, I remember, was burning and parched—
But for water or victuals we'd no time to stay,
He hurried us up so—we dared not delay.

The Emperor halted at length to take tea;
While he drank it, we rested awhile;—as for me,
I managed by chance to get hold of a cup,
And I felt like a wretch who a prize has picked up.

We'd not rested long, when we suddenly heard
The order to start:—at that ominous word,
Once more on all sides rose a hubbub and din;
What a hurry and scurry the nobs were all in!

The horsemen were not to such great hardships put,
But it *was* rough for those who'd to travel on foot;—
Are those fellows guards, or attendants, or what?—
Why some of them hav'n't a bow even got!

The swords of some men to their saddles are tied—
Not where they ought to be—girt to the side:

There is not such a thing as a cushion or pad*—
And of horses or men no "relief" to be had.†

The bearers, poor men, how they sweat, puffed and
  blowed,
As they trudged with the chair on the hot dusty road;
Still *he* was annoyed that they travelled so slow—
They *must* be more quick, if they drop as they go.

———

Tired and weary, our boots full of holes,
Some of them, too, being minus the soles;
Made only for show, they would fall off one's feet,
If, 'stead of a journey, one crossed but a street.

In crossing a river our thoughts soon would run
On what, in a former existence we'd done;
If we *had* a good action done once in a way,
We felt like a bearer who gets extra pay.

And wasn't it hard, too, to climb up a bank,
With the mud a foot deep, into which we all sank!

———

* Probably quilted pads laid from the chair to the
rooms the Emperor was to occupy.
† There ought to have been relays of horses and men at
every stage; this in the hurry had not been attended to,
or, perhaps, sufficient men and horses could not be mustered for the purpose. It is well known, too, that the
Emperor had to eat boiled eggs and the coarsest of food,
no preparations having been made to supply him with his
usual fare.

The slush on our feet never seemed to get dry,
For when! *this* stream was crossed, there was *that* one
    close by.

Still on we all went, and Shih-tsao soon appeared,
And *we*, tired and faint, the pavilion neared ;*
This, of all our long march was the pleasantest sight,
For here was our first halting-place for the night.

   The sun the hills pressed,†
   As we lay down to rest,
Not in soft beds, that was too great a treat;
   But wherever we found
   A nice bit of ground—
For we made a convenient bed of the street.

We were hungry as wolves, not a cash had we got
To have purchased the " bottoms " that stick to a pot;
Wouldn't a supper of some sort be nice?
I could have supped off the dregs of boiled rice.

As it was—those who got it—proceeded to cram
Their stomachs with maize—I got a raw yam,
Which I munched, as down on the bare ground I sat,
And was thankful to think I had got even that.

----

 * These are built at every stage from Peking to Jehol,
for the accommodation of the Emperor.
 † *i.e.*, the sun was setting.

How we sighed, as of home, wives and children we
    thought—
For by this time we all had a lesson been taught ;
The comforts of home *now* we thoroughly knew,—
And, were we safe back, could appreciate too.

There goes the first watch ; the moon overhead
Shines on all as we lie on our damp earthen bed ;
Who would have thought crimes committed by us,
Long forgotten, at last would come up with us thus !

So, *this*, then, is office and honours and rank—
Well, I *must* say, we've only ourselves got to thank ;
But of one thing I'm sure, had I earlier known
What I'd have to endure, I'd have let rank alone.

The second watch sounds ; the moon's sinking fast ;
I'm pierced to the bone by the cold autumn blast ;
Ah ! would I'd a blanket around me to fold !
But I've only a gauze coat to keep out the cold.

The third watch has sounded ; the moon now is set ;
The sky 's full of clouds—betokening wet ;
Not a sound breaks the stillness ; I hear not a tread ;—
Were I at home now, I'd lie snug in bed.

Not that I'm home-sick ; I don't funk or fret—
Thank goodness ! I'm not quite so bad as that yet ;
But *I must* own things seem to look pretty black,—
For the query is, when shall we ever get back ?

The fourth watch has sounded; now what shall we do?
It comes on to rain and we're all soon wet through;
If I'd only my waterproofs, then I'd not mind,
But alas! in my hurry I left them behind.

The fifth watch now sounds—other sounds, too, we hear,
For the dogs and the cocks bark and crow " dawn is
      near ; "
I'm worse now than ever; my eyes fill with tears,
Which I've scarcely wiped dry 'ere the daylight appears.

We tidied our clothes—that was very soon done—
To the front of the " travelling pavilion " we run,
Get ready the chair, and without more ado,
We start off again, just as if we all flew.

On the third morn at daylight we entered the hills;
Oh ! didn't we puff and get red in the gills !
Talk of roads—those we'd had were in sooth bad enough,
But—description fails here—in short, they *were* rough.

Range above range of mountains meet the eye,
Whose lofty summits spear the azure sky ;
Hills in confusion rise on every side,
Their distant tips with autumn's purple dyed.

This is *another* heaven ; the view from here
Is grandly beautiful. A rustic bridge
Spans a small mountain stream, whose waters leap

From rock to rock, till playfully they bound
Over a mimic precipice,—draping its face
With a transparent veil of liquid gems
Fringed with a bordering of sun-gilt spray.
Like words of love from half-reluctant lips,
It murmuring falls, and dies away in sighs
And gentle whispers as it nears the bridge
And glides beneath it on its sinuous way,
Its glistening face now glancing in the sun,
Now hid from view.

Our gaze was soon fixed on a glorious sight,
Which filled every bosom with pride and delight;
We forgot all the straits we'd till now struggled through.
As, stately and grand, the Great Wall loomed in view.

We thought how, in old times, its founder *Shih-huang**
Bestowed on brave *Mêng-chêng*—whose name lives in
    song—
A girdle of jade in the great olden hall,
For daring to follow her lord to the Wall.

But for beautiful scenes, or thoughts such as these,
We cared not; they could'nt our weary limbs ease;
Old white-bearded rustics we passed made us feel,†
The contempt they themselves took no pains to conceal.

---

* The "First Emperor."
† The old men on the road pointed at them with ridi-
cule, calling them cowards and runaways—it is presumed
not very loudly.

We jogged along rapidly early and late,
The hardships we suffered 'tis needless to state,
Suffice it to say we soon other hills passed,
Where the roads were more rugged and steep than the
    last.

Sometimes 'twas so steep we could hardly get on,
Ropes were tied to the chair and it had to be drawn;
What with pushing and pulling we sweat, puffed and
    blowed,
Till we'd got it well over a bad bit of road.

We whipped on our nags and continued our flight,
And arrived at Lan Piug on the 15th at night;
The round autumn moon shining brightly o'erhead,
Her silvery rays o'er ten thousand *li* shed.*

Each home has its offering of fruit, cakes and wine—
Had I been at home I'd have sure offered mine;
For there—in enjoyment my friends I should meet,
Here—I should like to get something to eat.

I've no one to talk to, so I raise up my eyes
To the bright moon, and heave some tremendous long
    sighs;
And I say to myself, "here's a plight to be in
Right or wrong, don't I wish myself back in Pekin!"

---

* The writer of this song, in spite of hardships, evidently
had an eye to scenery, etc.

Since I left home I've all sorts of hardships endured—
I couldn't be worse off I feel quite assured—
For I haven't so much as a cash in my pouch,
And for eight nights I've had the bare ground for my
    couch.

I would relish some wine, were it only a cup,
I really *do* think it would quite cheer me up,
And make me forget all my troubles ;—at least
It would help to get over the mid-autumn feast.

No such luck, so I threw myself down on the ground,
And was soon fast asleep—the next morning I found,
On awaking, the bright sun far up in the sky—
He'd commenced *his* day's journey, so also must *I*.

We got ready the chair and off we all ran,
Till 'ere long we neared the well-known river Lan,
The white waves were roaring and boiling like steam,
The ferry boat, too, was adrift down the stream.

We a floating bridge crossed to the opposite shore,
Which we all reached in safety—then trudged on once
    more,
O'er a long winding road,—many mountains we passed,
Till we saw to our joy Jehol's pailow at last.*

---

* Memorial arch.

Soon we got in the thick of the bustle and row—
Shops for medicine, tea, wine, tobacco, *yang yao ;**
It beat all the places I'd ever been in,
And put me in mind of Pouch Street in Peking.†

———

Gawky, white-hatted rustics, as clumsy as bears,‡
Went staring about—pedlars hawking their wares—
Old and young, rich and poor, men, women and boys,
Seemed to try who could make the most horrible noise.

Small paper umbrellas were hung at each door,
A proceeding I'd never heard tell of before ;
Why hang them up there I'm sure I can't say—
Our women would think 'twas the 35th day.§

Through hubbub and noise we continued our march
And shortly we passed the Memorial Arch ;

———

* Opium.
† Outside the " Front Gate " of Peking are two semi-
circular streets or arcades, where miscellaneous articles
both for use and ornament are sold ; these might reason-
ably be termed " Fancy Bazaars." They are called respectively East and West Pouch Lane.
‡ *Lit.* " Spoonies."
§ On the 35th day after a death, paper money is hung
at the doorways previous to being burnt. I cannot ascertain why umbrellas were hung up ; the custom must be
peculiar to the place, as must be some others I have met
with.

The palace was there; we drew near by degrees—
How even and nice looked its *chevaux-de-frise!**

It really looked handsome, majestic and grand,
In the midst, just before us, three lofty gates stand;
I can see, written over the great central one,
Three large golden characters thus : Li chêng mên.†

I hear that the grounds are quite forty *li* round,
In their precincts the green fir and cypress abound;
That 'neath their dark shade roam myriads of deer—
For no hunter dare think of disturbing them here.

At the gate all the nobs are drawn up in two rows,
And the chair smoothly‾enters 'midst many kotows;
What takes place inside I'm not able to state,
But what the guards did I'll proceed to relate.

We were all very tired and hungry, and dry;
Our clothing disordered, our hats all awry;
Our faces with sweat and with dirt were besmeared—
I must say a clean-looking lot we appeared.

---

* 轄罕木 *Hsia-kan-mu*, a word derived from the Manchu. These are three or four feet in height, made of wood, and placed on both sides of the entrances of palaces, yamens, etc.

† 麗正門 might be translated "Beautiful principal gate."

Off we went in small groups to look out for cribs,
Having beds rather softer than ground to the ribs ;
Some hunted up friends where they lodgings could get,
Some hunted up people with " Lodgings to let."

The dames knew their business and made a good squeeze,
But they managed to make us feel quite at our ease ;
They didn't use powder, cosmetics—what not—
But each on her neck a large *goitre* had got.*

We were told off to duties—not distressingly hard—
For we didn't mind now and then going on guard ;
What with one thing and t'other the time slipped away,
And 'ere long we got, what we wanted—our pay.

When the weather grew cold there were somewhere about
Three thousand fur coats—(dog and fox skin) served out—
Or they *ought* to have been ;—we were nicely sucked in—
They were sheep—made from myriads of pieces of skin.

Ere long, from Peking we received an express,
Stating they were all safe and well out of the mess ;
Entreating the monarch to come back post-haste,
And once more the pleasures of government taste.

A day was appointed on which to go back ;
It came, but all of us looked pretty black,
When told 'twas postponed, we'd got longer to stay,
The Emperor now having altered the day.

---

* I am told that nearly every second woman has that
unsightly swelling ; it is attributed to the water.

He didn't apparently feel half-inclined
To return—for he never could make up his mind:
'Twas " *yes* " at one moment, the next it was " *no ;* "
One day it was " *stop here,*" the next it was " *go.*"

He concluded at last he had better stay here,*
Pass the winter in quiet and go back next year;
His departure to Peking was too long delayed,—
He died, and his corse to Tung-ling was conveyed.†

---

* He was persuaded to stay by his Ministers, who probably dreaded he would be compelled to give audiences to foreigners, and thus become enlightened as to the doings of the mandarins.

† One of the family burial places of the reigning family. The other is Hsi-ling. Curiously enough, in this dynasty no Emperor is buried in the same place as his father; consequently, the Emperors are buried at Tung-ling and Hsi-ling alternately—Thus *Hsien-fêng* was buried at Tung-ling; *Tao-kuang* at Hsi-ling; *Chia-ching* at Tung-ling; *Chien-lung* at Hsi-ling; *Yung-chêng* at Tung-ling; *Kang-hsi* at Hsi-ling; *Shun-chih* at Tung-ling. The story goes that the effigy only of *Shun-chih* was buried at Tung-ling, though *he* privately retired to Wu-tai-shan, and became a priest. Numbers of Tatars go there annually to worship at the place on that account.

THE STONE LIONS OF LU-KOU BRIDGE.*

Should the traveller go
To the bridge of Lu-kou—
Distant from Peking about thirty *li*;
When once he gets there
If he 's leisure to spare,
He'll no doubt a wond'rous phenomenon see.

---

* Lu-kou bridge, 橋 溝 瀘, is distant from Peking about 30 *li*. It lies in a westerly direction from the Chang-i gate, 門 儀 彰. A stone road, made by *Liu-chin*, 瑾 劉, a eunuch of the Ming dynasty, leads to, and terminates at the bridge, which is much older than the road, having, it is supposed, been built during the T‘ang dynasty.

It is the general belief that no one has ever succeeded in counting the stone lions on the parapets at the sides of the bridge—though it seems a very easy undertaking.

For,—on either hand,
Some stone lions stand—
Or squat—or recline—on the parapets mounted ;
The number's not great,
Yet, strange to relate,
No mortal has ever those stone lions counted.

Of the many who've tried,
Some have sickened and died ;
Some have gone raving mad in the frantic endeavour—
Some count on day by day,
'Till they grow old and grey,—
But no one succeeds should he count on for ever.

Many persons have wondered,—
As there seems scarce a hundred—
That the task should be one of such very great labour ;
They may sneer and pooh-pooh it—
Let one try to do it—
He'll soon find himself just as bad as his neighbour.

One expert fellow hit on the plan of first pasting a piece of red paper on each side of the stone lions and afterwards counting them, but he is said to have died, leaving his task unfinished. Every one in the neighbourhood of Peking knows the legend, and many attempt to count the lions, but all have given up the task as hopeless.

Down the first row
He will carefully go,
And fancy he 's counted correctly, when, lo!
He's about to cross to the opposite side,
When every lion seems multiplied;
Where he had seen but one lion before,
Now he could easily count up a score.

Stone lions of every shape and size,
With tufted tails and tawny eyes;
Which seem to blink in the rays of the sun,
As if they were real and relished the fun.
Some, complacently licking their jaws—
Others as busily sucking their paws—
Little ones climbing up big one's backs—
Peeping from crannies, nooks and cracks—
Perched on the top of a parent's nose—
Stealthily peeping from 'twixt his toes—
At the top or the bottom, here or there,
Lions seem cropping up everywhere—
Under a belly—perched on an ear—
In the queerest of places the lions appear—
'Neath the tuft of a tail—'mong the hair of a
    mane—
You may strive to count 'em, but counting's in
    vain,
For you never can count the same number again.
No matter how often the victims count—
They may fancy they've got the exact amount—
They'll just run over once more and see,
When they find an alarming discrepancy;

One lion less here—one too many there—
At length they give the task up in despair—
Unless, as, alas! is too often the case,
They *must* go on counting and not quit the place,
'Till the counter eventually gets deranged,
Or dies, and at last to a lion is changed;
      Adding one more
      To that terrible score,
And making the counting more hard than before.

Whatever you do, or wherever you go,
Beware of the lions of stone at Lu-kou!
Don't try to count them—as sure as you do,
You'll die, become mad, or a stone lion too.

THE SKELETON TREES *

OR THE SUICIDES' HAUNT.

Do you see those old fir trees, dead, bloodless and dry—
  Like so many skeletons, bony and gaunt—
With their long fleshless arms stretching up in the sky?—
  'Neath those skeleton trees is the " Suicides' Haunt."

The wayfarer foredoomed to pass there at night,
  Hurries by with a shudder nor once turns his head ;
Nor feels himself safe till they're lost to his sight—
  Those skeleton trees are such objects of dread.

---

* These trees are situated on the east side of the Imperial Ancestral Hall, 皇 堂 子, near the British Legation, Peking. It is a common remark, if any one is seen walking beneath them, that he is " selecting a branch."

THE SKELETON TREES.

When they died no one knows, but old people say
  They were *blasted* because of the fruits that they bore;
But though they've been dead now this many a day
  The branches still bear their grim fruit as before.

Some men like to walk 'neath those old trees and brood—
  They are easily known by the scowl on their face,
For they all seem unhappy and fretful in mood :—
  They're the fruit of those trees and are ripening apace.

Night after night they will pace to and fro
  'Neath the skeleton trees, with sad lowering brows—
And their thoughts become dark, till they feel they must
    go
  And meet with their fate 'mong those leafless old
    boughs.

Sometimes every branch of those wierd looking trees
  Fills the night air with outcries, so like human screams,
That the passer-by feels his blood curdle and freeze—
  Those agonized shrieks haunt him long in his dreams.

'Tis said if a wayfarer passes by late,
  Gentle voices around seem to breathe in his ear,
" Climb up in the tree "—till, impelled by some fate,
  He feels that he *must*, and he slowly draws near.

He looks upward, and what a strange sight meets his eye,
  On every old limb fairy forms he can see ;
Could he only join *them*—there seems no one nigh—
  He *will* try, and climb up the skeleton tree.

Nearer, still nearer—he's ripening fast—
  Now he hastily climbs, and the morning sun flings
His rays on the fruit which has ripened at last—
  For a corse pale and swoll'n from a bony limb swings.

Whatever we do then, let this be our prayer—
  May *He* guide our actions and thoughts so aright
That we shun those old trees and the grim fruit they
    bear—
  God keep us from wishing to walk there at night.

LEGEND OF THE CHING DYNASTY.

———◁▷———

Shun-chih,* while yet a petty Tatar chief,
 Was down to everything—but few could match him,
A cross between a monarch and a thief—
 The Chinese General *Têng*† was sent to catch him;
Subdue his rabble horde—and, to be brief,
 Quiet *Shun-chih*, in other words, despatch him.

With this praiseworthy motive off *Têng* went
 To catch *Shun-chih*; should he succeed in taking
This noted chief, 'twould be a great event,
 In his own mind he rapid plans was making
How he could thrash him to his heart's content,
 And, for the future, stop his head from aching.

———————————————

 * 順治 *Shun-chih*. The first Emperor of the Ch'ing
(present) dynasty.
 † 鄧將軍. General *Têng* was sent into Manchuria to
subjugate *Shun-chih*, who was a great source of annoyance
to the last Emperor of the Ming dynasty.

Têng and *Shun-chih* in turn their skill displayed;
    Têng fancied he was smart—*Shun-chih* was smarter—
To catch the catcher he at length essayed;
    Firmly resolved on making him a martyr,
An artful trap for his opponent laid,
    And caught him, but the Chinese proved a Tatar.

Shun-chih felt quite delighted when he found
    His plan succeed; the man he so much dreaded,
Was brought into his presence tightly bound—
    In fact, the thongs were in his flesh embedded—
Seeing the general, *Shun-chih* grimly frowned,
    And ordered him at once to be beheaded.

No sooner said than done; a dexterous chop
    Aimed by a man at feats like this deemed clever,
Swept off his head; they saw the *head* fall flop,
    And looked to see the *body* fall, but never
Were men so taken in; it *wouldn't* drop—
    The headless trunk stood bolt upright as ever.

Here was a pretty mess; do what they would,
    They *couldn't* make it fall. This was appalling—
To give them credit they did all they could,
    But it defied their pulling and their hauling;
They pushed and pulled their best, but there it stood;
    The headless body didn't think of falling.

LEGEND OF THE CHING DYNASTY.

At his wits' end, *Shun-chih* tried tears and prayers,
    And various diplomatic arts to shake him;
If he'd but lie down he should be his Lars—
    His household god—his Ancestor he'd make him—
He'd worship him—he and his lawful heirs
    For ever—if he didn't, might the devil take him.

A moment scarcely had the words been spoke,
    When flashed the lightning and the thunder rumbled;
A moment more, the magic spell was broke,
    Down to the ground the headless body tumbled;
'Twas too late now his promise to revoke—
    He buried him, and left, crest-fallen, humbled.

He'd caught his Tatar with a vengeance now,
    His very ancestors he had repudiated;
Henceforth he yearly must with reverence bow
    At the ancestral tablet* of a man he hated—
He'd no alternative but keep his vow,
    No matter how absurdly it originated.

---

  * The tablet is placed in the Imperial Hall, 皇堂子, *Huang-t'ang-tzu,* and to this day the Emperor sacrifices before it on new year's eve; this seems to give much satisfaction to the Chinese portion of the population of Peking, though it may be questioned whether the Tatar portion are as much gratified. Whether the above legend is true or not is left to the opinion of the reader; it is, however, generally believed in Peking.

  This legend the Chinese treat, in a comic style as best expressive of their glee at seeing their conquerors outwitted.

He kept his vow—it does seem rather queer—
    It touches up their pride and helps to lower it—
From then till now, the last night of each year,
    The Emperor must sacrifice and kneel before it;
Much as our Tatar conquerors may sneer,
    It still remains a fact, they can't ignore it.

THE PALACE OF GOLD.

Dear Aunt, were sweet Ah-chiao my bride, I would bear
    her
    From this court and its pomp to some far away scene ;
There, secluded, shut out from the world, I'd prepare her
    A home worthy of her, and make her its queen.

Embosomed in hills, their blue summits uprearing,
    The edge of the horizon, forming a dome
Of the blue sky above us, the mountains appearing
    The natural many-hued walls of our home.

Like the sunshiny tears which trickle unbidden
    From the bright eyes of youth ; down the face of the
        hills,
Now catching the sun, now 'midst foliage hidden,
    In their sinuous course trickle numberless rills.

These streams from all sides are eternally flowing,
     Till they mingle their tears in a lakelet's pure breast,
On whose margin trees and sweet flowers are growing,—
     There, nestled in verdure, they placidly rest.

'Midst birds, flowers and trees, in the bright sunny weather
     She should never know sorrow, and never grow old
In the midst of the lake we'd live happy together,
     For *there* I should build her a palace of gold.*

---

    * *Wu-ti* 武 帝 of the Han dynasty, when quite a child, was asked by his aunt, princess *Chang* 長 whether he would like to marry. He replied, "Yes." On being shown *Ah-chiao,* Chang's daughter, and asked whether he would like to marry her, he replied, "If I had Ah-chiao for my wife I would build her a palace of gold."

THE SQUARE IRON BAR OF LU-KOU.

How came that great iron bar at Lu-kou ?
    Who placed it there—
In the bed of the river ?   Does any one know
    The reason it's square ?

'Twas the spear of a blood-thirsty pirate, 'tis said—
    By name *Wang-yen-chang;* *
If he could whirl that iron bar round his head,
    He must have been strong.

---

* *Wang-yen-chang*, 王 燕 章, was a notorious pirate in the T'ang dynasty; he used to levy a sort of "black mail" on all passing vessels, and was much dreaded on account of his enormous strength. The name of the person who killed him is not given in the legend, but there is no doubt the death of the giant was hailed with great joy by everyone.

The square iron bar remains in the bed of the stream to this moment—as far as I am aware—and is believed to be immovable by mortal hands. I question, however, if it would stay there long if any real efforts were made to pull it out. The Bridge of *Lu-kou* is the scene of two curious legends, the " Stone Lions," and the above.

He used that square bar both as weapon and oar—
  In rowing or fight.
In mid-stream he'd thrust it—his barge to it moor,
  When resting at night.

One night at the bridge of Lu-kou he had moored,
  And quietly slept;
When his foe, with a knife 'twixt his teeth, swam on
  board,
    And stealthily crept

To the place where the giant was taking his rest—
  Perhaps in a dream—
Drove his long knife right up to the hilt in his breast,
  And plunged in the stream.

The giant sprang up, with an unearthly yell—
  In pursuit of his foe ;
And, blinded by rage, on the top of him fell—
  Both sank down below.

Who can tell the wild struggle they had 'neath the wave—
  How each of them sought
The throat of the other—what death-blows they gave—
  How fiercely they fought ?

Clasped in death they were found the next morn near the
  spear
    In the stream's pebbly bed ;
Like wild-fire the joyful news spread far and near
  That the pirate was dead.

The square bar remains in the stream to this hour—
And there it must stay—
Where the giant had stuck it, for no earthly power
Can take it away.

RACE FOR A THRONE.*

" Thou on thy mule and I on my steed,
  Will try our animals' mettle and speed,
  In a *race* for the throne, and our course shall be
  Round " Nine *li* Hill " and back to this tree.
  He the imperial throne shall fill
  Who first makes the circuit of Nine *li* Hill,

---

* *Liu Pang* 劉邦 and *Pa Wang* 霸王, after many encounters, in which victory alternately favoured each of them, agreed to settle their dispute for the throne, by a trial of speed of the animals they respectively rode. The course was to be round " Nine *li* Hill," 九里山 called by that name from the fact of its being nine *li*, or three miles, round. The winner of the race was to be considered the lawful monarch, and the loser to consider himself as his subject, and tributary to him. When nearing the starting place *Pa Wang's* mule was taken in travail, and compelled by nature to stop and foal, thus preventing *Pa Wang* from winning the race.

Chief against chief, mule against steed;
Say, is't a bargain?" "Agreed! agreed!"

Between *Liu Pang* and the brave *Pa Wang*,
The struggle had been both fierce and long;
Each with ambition's flame was fired;
Each to the " Dragon throne" aspired;
Each had alternately lost and won,
In the race for power they had hitherto run:
Now, the struggle for power and place
Their beasts would decide in the nine *li* race.

Croupe to croupe were the two beasts placed,
Eastward and westward the riders faced;
One! Two! Three! and away they bound,
The hoofs of the animals spurn the ground,
In opposite courses each swiftly flies,
Each rider intent on the glorious prize.
In truth 'twas a trial of speed and skill
That race for the throne round Nine *li* Hill.

Gallopping on with clatter and din,
Eager the glorious prize to win,
On they go at the top of their speed,
Pa Wang on the mule, *Liu Pang* on the steed.
Who shall the fortunate rider be
That first gets back to the starting tree?
Each one mentally swears he will
Be first in the race round Nine *li* Hill.

" Faster, still faster, my trusty steed,
A kingdom rests on thy strength and speed."
" On, my brave mule, 'tis thou alone
Canst win for thy master the ' Dragon throne.' "
The mule or the steed, which shall it be
That first gets back to the starting tree ?
Which one will his master's hopes fulfil
And win the race round the Nine *li* Hill ?

Eastward and westward, back to back
Each man had sped on his lonely track ;
Now, as each rounded the hill in the race,
'Twas westward and eastward—face to face.
On they come at the top of their speed,
Pa Wang on his mule, *Liu Pang* on his steed ;
They meet—one half of the race is run ;
They pass—by whom will the race be won ?

Rounding the hill at the top of their speed,
Westward and eastward come mule and steed,
Impelled by their riders they seem to fly ;—
Yonder's the tree, they are both drawing nigh :
Fly, my brave steed, and be first at the tree !
On, trusty mule, all my hopes are in thee !
Who shall be first at the starting place—
Will the mule or the steed win the Nine *li* race ?

One effort more, and, my steed, thou hast won
For thy master the throne of " all under the sun !"

Alas! the poor mule, within sight of the goal,
Staggered—suddenly fell, and—gave birth to a
    foal!
"Brave steed! thou art first at the tree!" cried
    Liu Pang,—
"Curst mule!* thou hast lost me the throne!"
    cried *Pa Wang;*
"Accurs'd be thy race! they shall never more breed,†
But henceforth he foaled from the donkey and
    steed!"

---

  * Some books speak of the animal that *Pa Wang* rode
as a *t'é,* 特, and describe it as cloven-footed, and of surpassing swiftness. Others simply mention it as a mule.
Many dictionaries define *t'é* as a bull, bullock, or ox. "I
came as quickly as possible," "I went with the utmost
rapidity," etc., is often expressed by the words "I rode the
chasing wind *t'é*" 我騎的是追風特.

‡ 永不准下駒. "Never be allowed to foal."

THE ASPEN, OR, THE LAUGHING TREE.

Ha! ha! how I laugh when I see such a tree
    As the Elm to ambition aspire;
        He!—a poor worthless thing,—
        He to be dubbed a king! *
    What's there about *him* to admire?
        Just look at us both—
            Compare him with me;—
        As for beauty and growth,
           A mere tyro can see
    That I'm greener and stouter and higher;
And I know I'm more handsome and stately than he.

---

* It is said that the Emperor *Ch'ien-lung*, 乾 隆, greatly admired the elm tree, 椿 樹 (an inferior kind of tree to the 榆, or elm proper), and conferred on it the title of "king of the trees." It is a curious fact that, though the Chinese consider the tree comparatively worthless, and

Poor old Mulberry there, how he chafes, fumes and frets,
   And trembles in every limb,
      Till he reaches that stage,
      When he bursts with sheer rage,*
That Elm is made king over him.
    The mulberry tree
      But a poor pattern sets ;
    He should imitate me—
      He who laughs soon forgets.
I laugh at *Chien-lung's* absurd whim ;†
Ha! ha! that's the way to check useless regrets.

Willow weeps, Chestnut wails, sweet *kuai*‡ softly moans,
   And bitterly dark Cypress sighs ;
      Let the breezes but stir
      The branches of Fir,
   And the sturdy old tree howls and cries.
    Bluff Oak breathes despair

---

make no hesitation in grubbing it up to be used as fire-wood, yet, at the same time, no house is considered lucky, if a portion, often no bigger than a pencil, is not fixed in the roof at the building of it, generally in the form of a peg. This is recognizing its rank as king.

* The mulberry tree is supposed to exhale a great deal of vapour, and to burst with rage (氣破肚子), at seeing a worthless tree exalted over it, while the mulberry is considered so valuable, as affording subsistence to the silkworm.

† Alluding to his conferring the rank of king on the elm.

‡ A sort of ash, very beautiful both in foliage and blossoms, and useful in a variety of ways.

In lugubrious tones ;
Cherry, Apple and Pear
Commingle their groans ;
Shy Peach blushes up to the eyes.
Plum and Apricot's tears would melt their own stones.

Each tree of the forest, fruit, flower—great or small,
Is convinced that none other than he
Should be King of the Trees :
Let them think what they please,
But it has no effect upon me ;
I pursue my own way,
Let whatever befall ;
I'm contented and gay,
So I laugh and grow tall,
For of envy I'm perfectly free ;
Thus I'm really the king, and can laugh at them all.

Ha ! ha ! how I laugh as I gaze down below,
And watch the strange freaks of the sun
Gilt-edging the shade
My green leaves have made,
As hither and thither they run.
Just a cursory glance,
Through my branches bestow ;
How my leaves wave and dance,
And sway to and fro ;—
They are *clapping together in fun*
At the fanciful sun-bordered shadows they throw.

I laugh at the clouds, at the blue summer sky
   I laugh at the birds in their flight;
     At the sun overhead,
     Whose bright beams are shed
  On *my* head from morning till night.
   I laugh at those trees
      Which howl, whine and cry,
    For spring's gentlest breeze,
      Which makes *them* all sigh—
  Makes *my* leaves vibrate with delight—
That's my laughter!   What tree then so joyous as I?*

---

* The Aspen is supposed by the Chinese to laugh heartily (楊樹哈哈笑,) at the conceit of the elm, the anger of the mulberry, and the lamentations of the other trees, at the idea of the elm being considered their king. At the same time he evidently thinks himself infinitely superior, by his size and height, to the whole of them, and can afford to laugh at them all.   In this song, the Chinese poet shows the aspen in a different light from what foreigners generally view it.   One of our poets (Gay) in speaking of it says:—

  "Nor aspen leaves confess the gentlest breeze."

A favourite English ballad is named after its first line, which runs thus:—

  "Come where the aspens quiver."

We have also the common expressions, "*trembled* like an aspen," "*shook* like an aspen leaf," etc.

THE EMPEROR'S TREE.*

Not far from Peking is an old White-nut Tree ;—
Surrouuded by firs—that one tree stands alone ;
'Tis exactly the age of the Ch'ing dynasty,
For 'twas planted when *Shun-chih* ascended the throne.

Though hoary with years, its green-foliaged head
It sturdily thrusts up far into the sky,
As if in defiance of age,—for, 'tis said,
While the dynasty lives the old tree cannot die.

---

* 帝皇樹 This tree is in the courtyard of a temple
named Tau chê ssu 潭 拓 寺 situated in the Western Hills
about a hundred *li* from Peking. The above legend is
firmly believed by all northeners ; many Chinese making
pilgrimages to, or visiting the temple, going through the
kou-tou in front of it, in recognition of the awful power it
is supposed to possess. The tree is about six feet in
diameter ; at the root of it are several shoots (the song

Old age, storms, and time have attacked it in vain,
Yet year after year it bears foliage and fruit.
The death of a king, or a new monarch's reign,
Is foretold by a sapling that springs from its root.

Should *that* sapling droop, 'tis a monarch's death-knell;—
It it die, 'tis a sure sign the Emperor's dead;—
When a new monarch rules, on the spot where it fell,
Another green sapling springs up in its stead.

Each Emperor carefully watches the growth
Of the sapling which represents *him*, for he knows
That what affects *one* must be felt by them *both*;
That *he* cannot die while the sapling still grows.

The old tree is known as "The Emperor's Tree,"
And the sapling which now stout and thriving appears
At its foot, is *Tung-chih*.* Heaven grant we may see
The tree and its shoot flourish myriads of years!

---

gives but one), each of which represents one of the
monarchs of the Ch'ing dynasty, commencing with *Shun-
chih*, the first. *Hsien-fêng's* sapling was always a weakly
one, which was one more proof of the tree's power, as that
monarch was not celebrated either for mental or physical
strength. The present emperor's sapling looks thriving,
as the song says: how it may progress remains to be seen.
At the end of the Chinese version of this legend, affirmatory
of its truth, are the characters 定不虛言.

* Dead, since the above verses were written.

YU-CHI'S DEATH.*

—◦◦—

"It cannot be; say that you spoke in jest.
 Desert me—thus? Why turn your eyes away?
Oh! rather plunge your sword into my breast
 Than leave me here, to '*Han's* fierce troops a prey!

"Have I not shared your dangers hitherto?
 In darkest hour did I e'er quit your side?
Death in a hundred forms I've dared for you!—
 Ere I heard *this*, oh! would that I had died!

---

* *Yü-chi* (虞 姬) was *Pa-wang's* (霸 王) favourite concubine, and had followed his fortunes faithfully for years.
Pa-wang, on the desertion of his troops, told her he should
be compelled to leave her, as it would be impossible for
her to accompany him in cutting his way through the
troops that surrounded him. That she need be under no
apprehension, as her life would, no doubt, be spared when
they saw how beautiful she was. She, however, preferred
death by her own hand, in the presence of the man she
loved, to his desertion, and the certainty of falling into the
hands of his enemies.

" How oft in happier times you've sworn to me,
  Nor time, nor death itself should sever us !
Is *this* your boasted love ? Is this to be
  The bitter end ? Must it be really thus ?

" Have I not fought for you,—and near you bled ?
  And, oh ! how oft, while you securely slept—
My breast the pillow for your wearied head—
  The long night through I've faithful vigil kept.

" Have I not staunched your wounds with tenderest care,
  And wiped the sweat-drops from your clammy brow ?
Buoyed you with hope when you have felt despair ?—
  And could you, if you loved me, leave me now ?

" Let me go with you ; woman though I be,
  I'll side by side with you fight through this horde ;
I fear not death nor danger—they shall see
  How I, inspired by love, can wield a sword.

" What if I fall, 'twill be ' before your horse ; '
  My dying eyes can watch you in the fight ;
My soul, abandoning my senseless corse,
  Shall hover near and guard you in your flight.

" Recall your words, I earnestly entreat :—
  What, unrelenting still ! Thus then will I
Give up my life—here—at your very feet !
  'Twas my place living—at your feet I'll die ! "

4

Snatching *Pa's* glittering sword as thus she spoke,
    She plunged it in her breast; then looking round,
She faintly smiled—a cry the stillness broke,
    And *Yü-chi*, prone, fell dying to the ground.

" Said I not true?   See, yonder comes the foe!
    But yet you shall not leave me ere my breath
Has left this frame . . . Now—now, I bid you go!"
    She cried aloud, then closed her eyes in death.*

---

    * *Pa Wang* wept bitterly at her death, but there was no time for unavailing grief. Mounting his horse, he succeeded in breaking through the ranks of his foes, and fled in the direction of the Black River.

THE MOVING FIR.*

Just bow to that tree, be it never so slightly,
  And then a remarkable thing will occur ;
It at once will return it by bowing politely ;
  'Tis called for that reason the old Moving Fir.

It bends its head gently to all those who linger
  Beneath its dark shade, and its sympathy 's such,
If you place on its trunk but the tip of your finger,
  The whole of the tree will vibrate to your touch.

---

   * 活 動 松. This tree is in the court-yard of the Chieh-
tai temple (戒 台 寺), situated in the Western Hills
(西 山), about one hundred *li* distant from Peking. Many
foreigners have seen the tree, and can testify to the fact of
its moving when pushed with the hand ; readers may form
their own opinion about its politeness in the matter of
bowing, etc.

Now push it—it moves—one can scarcely conceive it—
  The whole tree bends down and recedes as you push;
It flies back to its place, when you let your hand leave it,
  As though it were merely a sapling or bush.

'Tis said,—tho' by some the strange tale is derided—
  That it *swings* o'er the depths of a cavernous well;
Trunk and roots by a thin crust of earth are divided;
  That the tree is suspended 'twixt heaven and hell.

That its roots, like its branches, are thrust into ether;
  That while the world lasts the old tree cannot fall;
Earth, hell, heaven, man—'tis dependent on neither,
  But, strangely enough, 'tis dependent on all.

What gives the old tree its strange power of volition?
  Some sprites have their home 'mid' its roots—old folk
    say;
When they're still, it remains in an upright position,
  But it bends when they tug at its roots in their play.

It now has defied storms and tempests for ages;
  When others are blown down, the old moving tree
Bends its head to the storm; when the wind wildly rages
  It rocks to and fro like a vessel at sea.

The tree is no fiction ;—'tis the truth I've related,
    And all who have seen it with me will concur,
That since *Pan-ku's* * time, when the world was created,
    The most wonderful tree is the old " Moving Fir."

---

* 盤古 the Chinese Adam.

SUICIDE OF PA WANG'S HORSE.*

"Alas! my brave black steed,
　　I grieve to part with thee;
　With strength and speed,
　In time of need,
　Thou'st borne thy lord,
　Through fire and sword,
　　Full many a thousand *li*.

"Thou'rt blacker than the night;
　　Matchless in symmetry;
　Whether in pursuit or flight,
　Dashing in the thick of fight,
　Thine eye ne'er lost its fire,
　Thy limbs could never tire,
　　Distance was nought to thee.

---

* *Pa Wang* presented the horse to *Ting-chang,* 亭長, the person who had charge of the boat, his only means of escape—as well to mark his appreciation of the man's

" My bravery to *thee* I owed ;
  My bosom knew not fear ;
While I thy back bestrode,
Fearless to the charge I rode ;
Oh ! steed, thy welcome neigh,
Eager for the coming fray,
  Never more I'll hear !

" Oh, steed !   My faithful black !
  I grieve to part with thee.
Ne'er more shall I cross thy back—
Ne'er more pat thy arching neck.
Thou wert true to me through all ;—
Take him—if but to recall
  Some memory of me."

Meanwhile the gallant horse stood up and drooped his
    haughty head,
As if he heard and understood all that his master said ;

———————————————————————————————

kindness as to prevent his horse from falling into the
hands of his enemies.   The horse like *Yü-chi*, 虞姬, *Pa
Wang's* favourite concubine—loved his master so well that
he preferred death to separation.

He nestled closer to his lord—and, oh! if eyes could
    plead,
How eloqueutly spoke the eyes of *Pa Wang's* noble steed.

They seemed to say reproachfully, " Why should we
    separate ?
" In life or death—whate'er befalls—I'd share my master's
    fate."
Pa Wang wept on the horse's neck.   " Poor steed," cried
    he, " thou'st shown
More love than all—thy noble heart's more human than
    my own.

"Take him away! I cannot bear that sad reproachful
    look."
Two soldiers, one on either side, the horse's bridle took,
And sought to lead him to the boat—in vain they kindness
    tried—
The horse indignantly refused to quit his master's side.

He fought and struggled fiercely,—and, not without
    remorse,
The men exerted all their strength to drag the panting
    horse ;
At last, o'erpowered by numbers, the horse, with drooping
    head,
Was slowly by his captors towards the river led.

They reached the stream ; the gallant horse gave a terrific
    bound ;
Broke from the guards who held him, and turning swiftly
    round,—
Looked fondly at his master—then, with one cry of pain,
He plunged into the river, and never rose again.

ONE-EYED LU-PAN, OR, COCKING THE EYE.

Have you ever observed a bricklayer at work—
  How knowing he'll look should a stranger stand nigh ?
How he'll step on one side, give his shoulder a jerk,
  Knit his brows, purse his lips, and then—cock his eye ?
  How knowing he looks, too, while cocking his eye!
      'Tis a curious fact,
      But you'll find it correct,
  All have the same habit of cocking the eye.

First he'll lay a few bricks, then, 'twixt finger and thumb
  He holds up a line—now, he's going to try
If his work is done straight—or, as workmen say, plumb—
  This is done in a moment by cocking the eye.
  It isn't the plumb-rule, its cocking the eye.
      He may try as he will ;
      Exert all his skill,
  But it cannot be done without cocking the eye.

In mixing up mortar, in handling a tool,
    He performs the same feat, but he won't explain why.
All his work should be tested by line and by rule,
    But he chiefly depends upon cocking his eye.
    It can't be correct without cocking the eye ;
            E'en in chipping a brick,
            He performs the same trick ;
    He can't chip a brick without cocking the eye.

Have you e'er seen a carpenter setting his plane,
    Which a knot in the wood has forced somewhat awry
How he taps till he gets the blade level again ?
    But the tapping 's no use if he cocks not his eye.
    It must be completed by cocking the eye ;
            He may tap for a week,
            But—the truth I now speak—
    'Twould never come right without cocking the eye.

Have you ever observed with what patience and care
    Stone-masons their mallets and chisels will ply ?
They oft try their work by the level and square,
    But they oftener test it by cocking the eye.
    They can tell when it 's square just by cocking the eye.
            They the level may use,
            Or the square, if they choose,
    But neither 's of use without cocking the eye.

Can *you* explain this? If *you* cannot *I* will:—
  In old times—or else all old chronicles lie—
There lived a poor artizan famed for his skill,
    Named *Lu-pan;* and this bricklayer had but one eye.
All know that old *Lu-pan* had only one eye;
      He had long lost the sight
      Of an eye—'twas the right—
He thus unavoidably cocked the right eye.

When old *Lu-pan* died, he was soon deified
  As the "Artizan's God," and that explains why
All workmen from that day to this take a pride
    In copying *Lu-pan's* peculiar eye.
They don't copy his *work*, they but copy his *eye;*
      Every one who would thrive
      Must earnestly strive
To imitate *Lu-pan* in cocking the eye.

Should a person inquire, "So and So — What 's his
    name,
  Is he a good workman?" If good—you reply—
Not that he 's skilful—you merely exclaim,
    "He 's a regular *Lu-pan* at cocking his eye!
He can beat even *Lu-pan* at cocking the eye!
      He does all he can
      To equal *Lu-pan,*
And attain to perfection in cocking his eye!"

In every respect what I've said is correct;
  Should any one doubt—he can easily try ;
The truth is soon proved,—but we must not expect
  To tell good from bad, for they all cock the eye.
If not skilful in *work*, they can all cock the eye ;
    Every one of them—all
    Good or bad—great or small—
  Are skilful in one thing, in—cocking the eye.*

---

* Many temples are dedicated to *Lu-pan* 魯班, who is generally represented in a sitting posture, having only one eye, and holding a square in his right hand. "Saint Lu-pan's Day" occurs on the 13th of the 6th Moon; on that day mechanics of all sorts proceed to his temple and offer propitiatory sacrifices to their patron deity.

Just within the P'ing tsê mên, 平則門, one of the gates of Peking, is a Lama temple called the White Pagoda Temple, 白塔寺廟; this was built in the reign of *Yung-lo* of the Ming dynasty. On its spire is an umbrella-shaped top, made of copper. In the first year of *Chien-lung's* reign the inhabitants of Peking were astonished one morning by discovering that this top had been ornamented by a red silk fringe, and that from it also were suspended a square, a bricklayer's trowel, and a plasterer's smoothing trowel. It was soon spread abroad that *Lu-pan* had descended from heaven during the night and performed the work, but had forgotten to take away his tools with him. It was subsequently discovered that the priests had obtained the services of a thief to do the work, and had circulated the tale of *Lu-pan* having done it, to draw contributions to the temple. *Chien-lung* punished the Chief Lama by depriving him of his rank (red button).

The tools are still to be seen suspended to the top, and, in spite of the trick having been found out and punished, such is the love of Chinese for the marvellous, that the Pekingese believe to this day that they were left there by *Lu-pan*, after repairing the temple.

MENG CHENG'S JOURNEY TO THE GREAT WALL.

In tracing back time's ever flowing stream,
I will not sing of heroes, war or glory;
A simpler subject far shall form my theme,
A woman's love—*Mêng Chêng's* pathetic story.

At once a wife, a widow, yet a maid,
No jade could be more pure, no snow be whiter;
The lustre of her name will never fade;
Ages have passed, it shines out clearer, brighter.

Couched in rude language though the tale may be,
To braver, nobler deeds you cannot listen;
Her journey to the Wall, ten thousand *li*,
Will cause the breast to swell, the eye to glisten.

My efforts will not altogether fail,
Should my rough verses but succeed in wringing
A tear or two from those who hear this tale,
Perhaps a sigh for those of whom I'm singing.

In Kuating city ages long ago,*
There lived, as local chronicles still show,
A man named *Mêng-lung-ti*, who, with his wife,
Passed many years an uneventful life,
Tranquil and happy, for no other care
Disturbed their peace, save that they had no heir;
Had they a child on whom their love to pour,
Then were they blessed, they craved for nothing
    more.

At length their fondest hopes were gratified,
The dame, with rising glow of conscious pride,
Announced herself, thanks to kind destiny,
The way all married ladies wish to be;
Ere long a little stranger blessed their sight,
Though but a girl, they hailed it with delight.
This child, e'en as the tendrils of the vine
Help to support the props round which they twine,
Would to their green old age new vigour bring,
And, by her love, support as well as cling.

---

* Upwards of two thousand years ago.

With joy, then, o'er this little pledge they hung,
And at the "full moon" named the child *Mêng
Chêng;**
Nor was it ever changed, the name they gave,
She bore in life, and carried to her grave.

Years passed, the little *Mêng Chêng* grew apace,
All hearts delighting by her childish grace,
Clever beyond her years, she passed her hours
In study, needlework, embroidering flowers.
In all accomplishments the girl excelled,
Charming her parents, who with pride beheld
Her industry, her kind and winning ways.
The neighbours too spoke loudly in her praise;
So beautiful, so skilful, yet so young,
Who was the equal of the fair *Mêng Chêng!*
The time rolled on, the girl was now sixteen.
In all her life her thoughts had ever been
How by her fond devotion day by day,
She could her parents' kindness best repay.
Like to a rosebud 'neath a genial sun,
Her budding charms unfolded one by one,

---

* The first name a child receives is called its " Milk
name," and is equivalent to our "Christian name."
Children can be named on any day after their birth, from
the 3rd to the 30th or "full moon" or "complete month."
The 3rd and 30th days after the birth of a child are the
favourite days for the ceremony of giving it its "Milk
name."

Each day developing some lovelier grace,
Rounding her form, and dimpling her fair face,
The young girl blossomed into maidenhood,
Fair to the eyes, yet not more fair than good.

Her birthday dawned : the happy parents blessed
Their blushing daughter, whom they thus ad-
    dressed :—
" You're now sixteen, as each revolving year
Rolls on, still ' sweet sixteen ' may you appear ;
May your young life be one continual spring,
And every added year new pleasures bring.
But yet my child—'tis written so by fate—
The time will come when we must separate ;
We both are old, and time steals slowly on,
Our care then is for you when we are gone.
You will be rich, all that we have is yours ;
But 'tis not wealth that always best insures
Content and happiness. We must provide
A fitting husband for so fair a bride ;
Invite a son-in-law to assume our name,*
This, for your sake, must be our highest aim ;

---

* A person having no male children, and not wishing
his family name to become extinct, can, if he choose, invite
a person to marry his daughter, which he does through
the medium of the go-between. On marriage, the bridegroom becomes a member of his father-in-law's family ;
the first son assumes his mother's maiden name, and
inherits the family property, his descendants doing the
same in perpetuity ; the remainder of the bridegroom's
children retain *his* name.

Graft our child's husband on the parent tree,
Your children then we yet may live to see.
What say you, child?" The blushing girl replied,
" Why should you wish to drive me from your side?
The thought of marriage only gives me pain,
Ah! rather let me ever thus remain,
To wait on both, and by increasing care,
Still, as of old, your fond affection share :
I'm but a child, then let me, I implore,
Stay as I am, what can I wish for more ? "

———

I'll not sing of Kua-ting or of *Mêng Chêng* now:
—That portion of my task's already done—
But of a couple living in Soochow,
On whom, in old age, heaven bestowed a son.

When three days old the child received his name,
'Twas *Wan-hsi-liang*—'tis in old records shown.
From then till death it still remained the same,
Never was he by any other known.

The child was beautiful beyond compare,
More like a fairy being who had played
With baby angels in the upper air,
And then unconsciously had earthward strayed.

5 *

His parents watched with love his rapid growth,
Each day developing some mental grace,
Which more endeared him to the hearts of both,
Than e'en the beauty of his fair young face.

When eight years old, he could repeat by rote
All the "Four Books," and the " Five Classics " too;
The sayings of the Sages he could quote :
Besides, he much of Ancient History knew.

When he had studied and had mastered those,
He next tried Essays.   These he wrote so well,
In composition, poetry or prose,
But few could equal, none could him excel.

———

I'll leave the boy thus, and the scene will transport
To the capital city, the emperor's court ;—
The frontiers long had been ravished by hordes
Of fierce mounted Tatars with spears and with
    swords.
The Emperor, thinking their inroads to check,
And fearing, perhaps, their wild troops to attack,
Called in to his aid many workmen well skilled,
And gave them directions a great wall to build ;
The wall was to be the whole country in length,
With towers and gateways of suitable strength.
This wall would his subjects in safety enclose,
And be an effectual check to his foes.

The work advanced slowly, at ruinous cost,
For myriads of lives in its building were lost;*
The dying and dead were enclosed in the wall,
No matter their rank, 'twas a vast tomb for all.

One night, on retiring, the Emperor dreamt,
In Soochow was a lad who from vice was exempt—
Who, whatever he did, or wherever he went,
Would a myriad of common-place men represent.†
The Emperor woke, and, elated and pleased,
Sent to Soochow *instanter* to have the lad seized.
Soochow's six gates were immediately guarded,
And every available spot was placarded.‡
In every alley and lane of the city,
People assembled with looks full of pity;
Many a murmur and shake of the head
Were heard and seen as the placard was read.

It ran thus:—" If anyone dare to conceal
The lad *Wan-hsi-liang*, he shall certainly feel
The law's direst terrors for treason so great;
He shall suffer beheading, a murderer's fate;

---

* It is unknown how many actually died in the building
of the " Great Wall," but they must have amounted to
many thousands; the Wall being the general tomb of all
who died there.
† The lad's surname was *Wan* 萬 " myriad."
‡ The advantage of bill-sticking was evidently known at
this early date.

The family shall also, of him who so dared,
Be cut off root and branch, not a soul shall be
    spared.
But, if, on the other hand, anyone know
Where *Wan* is concealed, and shall instantly go
And give such information as may at length lead
To his capture, he'll do a most praiseworthy deed.
And further, a handsome reward shall be paid
To the person or persons by whom it is laid;
And those through whose prowess the capture is
    made,
If official, shall each be promoted one grade."

When the father read this he was nearly distrait,
Tore his hair in despair, and cursed his sad fate;
" Why should he seek to rob me of my son?
Other fathers have many, while I have but one!
If my son is taken to build the Great Wall,
He will never return.   Losing him, I lose all.
On whom, save my son, can I hope to depend
For comfort and help as I draw near my end?
In old age or sickness who *but* him can soothe
My last dying moments, the road to death smooth?"
Bewailing his fate thus with sad tears and moans,
He at once hastened home, and in heart-breaking
    tones,
Imparted the news to his agonized wife,
And tremblingly bade his son fly for his life.
The wondering lad both his parents obeyed,
First bathing, and then in clean robes was arrayed;—

Sacrificed, with his parents, to Heaven and Earth,
To the Gods, and to those who had given him
    birth;—
To their ancestors' tablet, their forefathers' tomb,
Praying their manes to avert such a doom
As the one that hung over themselves and their
    son—
To guard him and them. The sacrifice done,
The poor weeping youth bade his parents not grieve,
Cried he, " 'Tis but for a short time I leave,
A few days or weeks and this crisis once o'er,
We'll all be united again as of yore."
Here the poor lad broke down, fondly looking at each
Through his tears, while deep sobs interrupted his
    speech.
" If I'm apprehended and die at the Wall,
On you both, in old age, this sorrow will fall.
Is't for this you both reared me? Oh! why was I
    born?
Oh! why must I leave you? Why from you be
    torn? "
With dreadful forebodings they'd never meet more,
Mid' sobbing and tears, the lad rushed from the
    door.

On he ran, with untiring feet,
On, through alley, and land and street;
Meeting many a face he knew,
But heedless of all he onward flew;
Turning neither to left nor right,
Till the gate of the city appeared in sight.

People to many a village belonging,
Coming and going to and fro,
In and out of the city were thronging.
Some seemed struck with his look of woe.
On through the gate of the city he sped,
And out through the open country fled,
For he knew that a price was set on his head.

Everyone on the road he met,
Eagerly asked, " Have they caught him yet ?
Living or dead, he's sure to be found,
He cannot escape if he's above ground ;
It wouldn't be pleasant to be in his shoes."
For everyone 'ere this had heard the news.
Over the dusty road he speeded,
Footsore and weary still he ran ;
Towns and hamlets he passed unheeded,
He dreaded to go near the haunts of man.
Over the dusty road he sped,
With wearied limbs and feet that bled,
For he knew that a price was set on his head.

Over the hot and dusty road,
On, the weary fugitive strode ;
Till, tired and faint, he suddenly spied
A garden wall close by the roadside ;
Farther on, a temptingly open gate.
Seeing no one near, he made for it straight.
The garden looked so cool and shaded
" Ah ! what a refuge 'twould be for me !
I'll venture ! "—at once he its precincts invaded,
And threw himself down at the foot of a tree.

Here, he in safety might pass the night,
Rise at the dawn and continue his flight,
With a body refreshed and a heart more light.

———

I'll leave the lad upon the greensward flung,
Weary and footsore, sad and sorrow-laden ;
And tune my muse once more to fair *Mêng Chêng*,
And sing of what befel the gentle maiden.

'Twas eventide, the sun was sinking fast,
And, as he sank down in his western bed,
His dying radiance o'er the landscape cast,
Tinging the foliage with a golden red.

Some remnants of his brightness still remained,
A filmy veil of glorious light and shade ;
As if, though out of sight, he still refrained
From taking *all* the glory he had made.

The fair *Mêng Chêng*, her daily task being done,
Tripped from the house and towards an arbour ran ;
To watch from thence the slowly setting sun,
Her taper fingers toying with a fan.

The bower stood on a gentle eminence,
Some twenty feet above the garden raised ;
She gained the summit, turning round from thence,
On sinking sun, and hill, and dale she gazed.

The scene enclosed within the garden wall—
The house, the bower, the lake so still and pure,
The flowers, the trees—the palms o'ertopping all—
Looked like a Paradise in miniature.

Green foliage on every side appeared,
Bright flowers bloomed in many a gay parterre;
The tufted palm its lofty head upreared,
High above cypress and the azure fir.

The playful beams, e'en though their lord had gone,
Still danced and flickered midst the topmost boughs;
Toying with every leaf they glanced upon,
Kissing at last the tall palm's stately brows.

On air and sky their impress next they showed;
Sunward their course they dancingly pursued,
Purpling and goldening the air, which glowed,
Becoming, through their influence, rosy-hued.

Embosomed in the midst of this fair scene,
Lay, mirror-like, a lakelet calm and clear,
Reflecting back its bordering of green,
The fleecy clouds, the glowing atmosphere.

High overhead, far in the vault of blue,
Rode the pale moon amidst the ambient air;
Her modest glances in the lakelet threw,
Seeing her own fair face reflected there.

Charmed by the beauty of the scenery—
The placid stillness of the lakelet's breast,—
She gazed upon it long and dreamily,
At length she thought she'd seek the bower and rest.

Each step she mounted, backward looks she cast
From thence, another point of view to take ;
When suddenly a gust of wind swept past,
Caught up her fan, and hurled it in the lake.

Loudly she called her maid, but no one came.
Finding at length she could not make her hear,
She thought, " Why need I feel false pride or
       shame ?
I'll fetch the fan myself ; there's no one near."

No sooner had the girl the thought expressed,
Than down the steps again she lightly ran ;
Looked coyly round, then hastily undressed,
Bent on obtaining back the truant fan.

She paused awhile, then, slowly turning round,
Her face and form became suffused with red ;
Her eyes in modesty, had sought the ground,
But rested on the lake's clear face instead.

And there she saw—as if ' 'twere sculpt' of stone—
An unclothed form, a living statuette ;
A fair young face,—she recognised her own,
And blushed a crimson when her own eyes met.

She gazed admiringly, yet bashfully,
As if she felt an innate sense of shame;
She *knew* she blushed, for she could plainly see
The rosy blood rush mantling through her frame.

As thus she stood, she chanced to raise her eyes,
'Ere stepping in the lake to get the fan;
But who can paint her horror and surprise,
When *her* eyes met the dark eyes of a man?

Yes, there, beneath the lofty palm-tree's shade,
There stood a lad, good-looking, tall and slim,
Intently gazing on the beauteous maid.
Her gaze in turn became transfixed on him.

The girl, with mingled modesty and fear,
Arrayed herself in haste as best she could;
She dared not look, she *felt* him drawing near.
'Ere she was clothed, the young man by her stood.

A man to see her *thus*, she was dismayed,
And could have sunk into the ground with fright;
Abashed, confused, perplexed, she yet displayed
Some anger too, as well indeed she might.

Yet, strange to say, there mingled with all this,
A pleasant feeling, hitherto unknown;
Making her bosom swell and glow with bliss;
Her bright eyes 'neath its influence brighter shone.

" I bless the chance," the smiling youth began,
" That led me here—a fugitive—to take
Shelter awhile ; but, oh ! I bless the fan,
Blown by the gust of wind into the lake !

" Ah ! but for that, my eyes had ne'er been blest
With such a vision as I've just surveyed ;
The sunset scene, the lakelet's placid breast,
And its presiding queen, a very naiad."

" Who are you ?   Whence came you ?   What is your
     name ? "
Cried the girl, as she reddened with anger and
     shame ;
" Who are your parents ?   Where do you dwell ?
" How came you hither ?—the truth at once tell."

Without hesitation, the lad told her all ;
How he was wanted to help build the Wall ;
The grief of his parents for whose sake he fled,
The placards announcing a price for his head.

How, wearied and footsore, impelled by kind fate,
He saw the flower-garden, and entered the gate,
Intending to rest 'neath the trees for a night,
And early next morning continue his flight.

He continued, " While resting my limbs in the shade,
I heard a sweet voice calling out for her maid ;
I looked whence it came and my glad eyes were blest
With a vision of beauty, and—you know the rest.

" You have heard my sad tale, I a fugitive stand ;
My liberty, life, all, are now in your hand ;
May I crave your permission one night here to stay ?
And to-morrow, at dawn, I'll proceed on my way."

The girl had alternately flushed and turned pale,
As the young lad related his pitiful tale ;
Then exclaimed, " You must never again quit this
       spot,
But share, with my parents and me, our poor lot.

" Who sees my fair form, as you did but just now,
Must make me his wife ; for I solemnly vow,
All the troubles and griefs he may yet have to bear,
As a true, loving wife I will faithfully share.

On my unclothed form your eyes just now gazed ; "
She here dropped her eyes, which before had been
       raised ;
" And I love you far dearer, far better than life ;
You *must* be my husband, I *must* be your wife."

On the banks of the lake then they sat side by side,
In fancy already a bridegroom and bride ;
They lingered awhile in the deepening shade,
And many a vow to each other they made.

Filled with visions of brightness they both prattled
    on,
Till growing night forced them at last to be gone;
They arose from the ground and ingeniously planned
To enter the house, as they stood, hand in hand.

———

Thus hand in hand and full of confidence,
Engendered by their youth and innocence;
They gained the house, and now with love grown
    bold,
The artless girl the whole adventure told.

His own heart warming to the handsome youth,
The father listened, seeing nought but truth
In their ingenuous faces, smiling said,
"So you are *Wan-hsi-liang*, and you have fled
"From those you hold most dear, from home and
    friends?
Stay with us here; we'll try to make amends
For all the wrong the Emperor has done;
Be my child's husband; be to me a son.

"Take her, she's all that I love here on earth;
Like me, you'll soon appreciate her worth.
I'm rich, on you my riches I bestow;
My greatest recompense will be to know
Two loving hearts will prop my failing age
Be near me, when I close life's pilgrimage."

" What," cried the lad, " would you your riches
    give,
Your daughter too, to me, a fugitive ?
Your only child on my acceptance press
Cause her to share my suffering and distress ?
Much as I love her, I could never dare
To blight the happiness of one so fair,
By linking my unhappy fate to hers,
Bethink you well, if such a thing occurs,
Would not the news on all sides quickly spread,
And soon bring dire misfortune on your head ? "

The old man cried, " Your safety I'll ensure
Stay in the inner rooms, there rest secure
Till this unfortunate affair 's blown o'er,
And you can safely show yourself once more."
Convinced at last, he'd nought to apprehend,
Loving the girl, and fearing to offend,
The youth no farther opposition showed,
But thankfully confessing all he owed
For the unbounded kindness they had shown
To him, a wanderer, homeless and unknown,
Agreed to everything ;—what next befel,
Time, and the following rhymes will clearly tell.

———

This very night shall the wedding be kept,
Of *Wan-hsi-liang* with the fair *Mĕng Chĕng ;*
Let the great hall be properly swept,
Garnished, festooned, and the flower-lamps hung.

Hurry and bustle both old and young—
Let the tapers be of the brightest red;
Emblems of joy for the fair *Mêng Chêng*,
And the youthful lover to-night she'll wed.

Alas, how often in worldly things,
Just when our prospects appear most bright,
An apparent trifle misfortune brings,
And our sunny morning is turned to night.

As nothing is hidden under the sun,
The news spread quickly far and wide;
The ceremony was scarcely done,
When clamouring voices were heard outside.

" Open the door!   We'll burst it in!
Where is the youth who hither fled ? "
Hoarse cries are heard 'mid the uproar and din,
" We'll have the bridegroom, living or dead."

The noise is increasing more and more;
" Hark to the angry voices without!
Hear, how our enemies batter the door,
Raising, at every blow, a wild shout."

" Hide, oh! hide, for your young wife's sake!
Hark, the rude voices are drawing near!
Here, in this store-room, shelter take—
They'll never think of finding you here."

6

The feeble door, alas, cannot stay
The efforts of those for blood athirst ;
'Neath continued blows it at length gives way,
Everyone striving to enter first.

Search was made for him here and there,
Search was made for him high and low—
Kitchen and closet everywhere
Wherever a human form could go.

In every room of the house they sought ;
At length in the store-room he was found ;
Into the hall the youth was brought,
His legs and arms being tightly bound.

Into his shoulder a spike was thrust,*
Causing the lad to writhe with pain ;
Like a joint of meat the poor lad was *trussed ;*†
His neck was bound with a heavy chain.

In this pitiful plight he stood in the hall ;
The old man cried, while the rest looked on,
" What shall I do when you go to the Wall ?
Who will console me when you are gone ? "

---

* A piece of iron or chain is thrust into the flesh,
passing under the collar-bone, and coming out on the
other side, where it is secured together. Prisoners are
often secured in that manner now.
    † *Lit.* " like a sausage."

Cried the youth, " When I to the Wall am borne,
I shall die, and my bride will again be free ;
She is young—let her not for my sad fate mourn,
She must strive to forget such a wretch as me.

" I carry misfortune wherever I go ;
Better by far that I should die ;
On some other lover her hand bestow,
And may he be happier far than I."

" Listen to me," was the girl's reply,
" You are my husband, I am your wife ;
Death cannot sever that sacred tie,—
A true woman weds but once in her life.

" The good horse is chary of turning his head
To graze off the ground he has just passed o'er ;
A faithful wife when her lord is dead,
Is true to him still ; she weds no more."

At length the time came to separate,
The bride from her husband's side was torn ;
He, to be dragged to a wretched fate,
She, his absence or death to mourn.

Even the bystanders felt for the pair,
And openly murmured their sympathy
For the new married couple so young and fair
Thus torn asunder through tyranny.

6 *

The road to the Wall was long and drear,
Day by day the lad weaker grew;
The end of his journey and life drew near,
When at length the Great Wall appeared in view.

Three days after the youth arrived,
He died, and the Great Wall became his tomb:
Flung in by those who yet survived,
Daily expecting a similar doom.

Months passed, the maiden daily grew more pale,
Her parents did the best they could to cheer her;
Their well-meant kinduess was of no avail,
Dear were they to her, yet her lord was dearer.

She *must* go to him—was she not his bride?
And was it not her duty to be near him?
In life or death her place was by his side:
If sick or dying, who but she could cheer him?

Her parents tried this strong desire to check;
Alternately they threatened and persuaded;
How could she travel that long dreary track?
What could she do, a girl, alone, unaided?

Firmly resolved on going to the Wall,
She left her parents almost broken-hearted;
She was his wife—to find him she'd brave all:
So on her long, long journey she departed.

Her dress was plain—no ornaments she wore,
Save a gold ring to show that she was married;
She'd have to beg her way from door to door—
For not a single cash the young girl carried.

————

On through alley and lane and street,
She tottered along on her tiny feet;
Meeting many a well-known face
As she was leaving her native place:
Hearing many a kind regret
That she was going, from those she met;
Hastily through Soochow she proceeded,
Turning neither to left nor right,
Noise and bustle the girl ne'er heeded,
Till the gate of the city appeared in sight
Many a wondering look was cast
On the lonely girl as she hurried past,
Till she cleared the streets of the city at last.

Through the gate of the city she pressed,
Pausing neither for food nor rest;
Over the dreary road she sped,
Heedless of what the wayfarer said,
Village and town the girl passed through,
Till at dusk she reached the pass of Hsü-shu.
Seeing the girl the guards demanded,
" Why are you out so late, my lass?
You can't have travelled here empty-handed,
So you'll treat us and then we'll let you pass.

You'd no business out ou the road so late ;
If you have no money you'll have to wait,
For we cannot allow you to pass the gate."

She turned to the guards with a bitter smile
" I have travelled to-day," said she, " many a mile ;
Alas! had I money, I'd cheerfully give—"
Here, seeing no other alternative—
She tore off her skirt, which she gave to the man,
" Take it, and pawn it for drink, if you can."
The person in charge of the barrier hearing
Some voices apparently wrangling, came out,
To allay all the hubbub ;—on his appearing,
He demanded to know what the noise was about.
Bidding the maiden at once relate
Why she was out ou the road so late,
And her motive for wantiug to pass the gate.

The trembling girl told the officer all,
How *Wan-hsi-liang* had been dragged to the Wall—
That she'd scarcely a moment become a bride,
When her husband was ruthlessly torn from her
    side ;
Home, parents, and friends, she had given up all
To follow her husband aloue to the Wall
The officer said, when the tale was related,
The truth of your story time only will show ;
He then bade the girl, who impatiently waited,

First sing " Names of Flowers,"* and then she should
go.
A moment's pause, and the night air rung
With the mellow voice of the fair *Měng Chěng*,
The guards clustered round her, as thus the girl
sung :—

SONG

1.

" 'Tis the first moon—'tis Spring: the red lamps are
lighted :
To hail the New Year, guests now meet in the hall;
Other husbands and wives in their homes are united,
My husband is taken to build the Great Wall.

2.

The second moon's come, and the swallow's are pairing;
How they twitter and chirp, as if proud and elate ;
'Neath the eaves their old nests they are busy repairing,
They all have their homes, and each has its mate.

---

* There is evidently a mistake here in the name of the
song. It ought to have been—by the tenor of her song—
" The Twelve Months." " Names of Flowers " is not the
name of a song, but of a favourite tune.

3.

'Tis the 3rd of the 3rd, the peach trees are blending,
Their rose-tinted hues with the willows' so green ;
Old and young to the tombs, to burn paper, are
    wending,
But none at the tombs of my people are seen.

4.

'Tis the fourth moon—'tis genial and mild sunny
    weather :
This is the time when the silkworms are bred ;
Maids and matrons the mulberry leaves go to gather :
They can't pluck them faster than my tears are shed.

5.

'Tis the fifth moon—rice-planting—wife, widow and
    maiden,
Every one, old and young, busy appears ;
The hot air with dampness and mildew is laden.—
My face is mildewed and moistened with tears.

6.

'Tis now the sixth moon—the heat is increasing,
The gold-speckled pailing's* too listless to sing ;
The hum of mosquitoes at night is unceasing,
My blood they may drink, so *he* feels not their sting.

---

* A species of thrush.

7.

'Tis the seventh moon—autumn's cool breezes are
    blowing;
At each open window and doorway are seen
The matrons and maidens all busily sewing
Their bright coloured garments of red, blue, and green.

8.

'Tis the eighth moon—the wild geese are overhead
    winging
Their way to the west; in old time it is said,
One, a token of love to a husband was bringing,—
But the bird at the feet of the husband fell dead.

9.

'Tis the ninth moon—husbands and wives are united;
On the ninth day each pledges the other in wine;
To view the chrysanthemums guests are invited;—
Shall I ever drink out of one cup with mine?

10.

'Tis the tenth moon—the farmers their rich crops
    in-gather;
The rustics are busy in every field;
They sing as they work in the bright golden weather,
And rejoice o'er their task in the bounteous yield.

11.

'Tis the eleventh moon—the snow-flakes around me are
    falling ;
The snow and the cold do not my heart appal ;
At night, in my dreams, I hear his voice calling,
He bids me, his wife, seek for him at the Wall.

12.

'Tis the twelfth moon—each household is busy pre-
    paring
To keep the New Year,—pigs and sheep are now slain ;
While I, to the far distant Wall am repairing,
Broken-hearted and sad till I see him again."

While the girl sung,
There was many an eye
That had long been dry
Moistened by tears,
Which, perhaps for long years,
Had never from one of those eyes been wrung.

Yes, those guards, unfeeling and rough,
For once in their lives made good use of a cuff ;
Who knows but that two or three tears such as
    theirs
Were just as efficient as long-winded prayers.

Her right to pass through they owned she had
 earned ;
And even her petticoat they returned.
The officer then bade them open the gate,
And let her pass even though it was late.
Bidding the barrier guards adieu,
In the darkness she shortly was lost to view.

On her journey the young girl sped,
With tottering limbs and feet that bled ;
Still she travelled on, day by day,
Having no money, she begged her way.
The poor girl's story like wildfire flew,
Every village she journeyed through,
People came thronging forth to meet her,
Women and children, old and young ;
Many a kindly word would greet her—
All would have willingly helped *Mĕng Chĕng*—
 She appeared in truth like the fair *Kuan yin,**
 The vilest man would have scorned the sin
 Of insulting so faithful a heroine.

Travelling many a weary mile,—
Sometimes pausing to rest awhile,—
Crossing many a river wide,—
Climbing many a mountain side,

---

 * The Goddess of Mercy.

As they gazed they saw with fear and wonder,
A tower that stood on the top of the Wall,
With a roar like thunder, rend asunder,
Sway for a moment, then topple and fall;
Disclosing, when dust and smoke had done,
The clothing worn by her husband *Wan*
Containing his ghastly skeleton!

———

The girl knelt down at the skeleton's side,
And, taking its hand, she the "*blood test*"* applied,
This at once would determine and palpably show
If 'twere really the corse of her husband or no.
Then she pierced her own hand and let the blood
    drop
On that of the skeleton, where, should it stop,
And congeal, or at once be absorbed in the bone,
That the corse was her husband's would plainly be
    shown,
If the blood from the hand of the skeleton ran,
Then the corse was not his but of some other man;
The true or false only the "blood test" could tell,
'Twould be his if congealed, not his, if it fell.
The workmen thronged round her, awe filled every
    breast,
At seeing the maiden apply the blood test;

———

* The "blood test" is applied, in cases similar to the
above, even at the present time.

A dead silence reigns on them all as they stand,
And watch her blood drop on the skeleton's hand,
That the bones are her husband's the test soon
　　　reveals,
For as fast as the blood drops, so fast it congeals.
Then she pulled off her skirt which she over it
　　　spread,
And mournfully sat herself down by the dead ;
And rocking herself to and fro by its side,
She bewailed his sad fate as she bitterly cried ;—
" Oh, my husband ! and was it for this that we wed ?
Have I travelled this distance to find you here dead ?
Ah ! why were you dragged here to build the Great
　　　Wall ?
May he who destroyed you in like manner fall !
Accursed be the monarch* by whom it was done !
May the tyrant's unburied bones bleach in the sun ! "

A magistrate chancing to pass at this time,
Heard the Emperor cursed ;—'twas so awful a crime
That he instantly went and made out a report
Of the case, which he took with his own hand to
　　　court.

---

* Southerners execrate the name of this Emperor, but
Northerners speak more favourably of him.

The Emperor's "dragon eye" glanced o'er the page,
Till he'd read its contents, then he trembled with
    rage ;
"What! one of my subjects to dare to asperse
Her sovereign's own acts, and her sovereign curse !
Bring the culprit before me, this case I will try,
And decide, when I've heard it, what death she shall
    die.
On her and her kindred my vengeance I'll launch,—
I'll exterminate all :—cut them up, root and branch !"

In a short time the girl to the palace was led,
And the crime she was charged with before her was
    read.
Mêng Chêng then knelt down in the great hall of
    gold,
And the whole of her tale to the Emperor told.
As she told her sad story the "dragon eye" shone
With a lustre surpassing the gems on his throne ;
He had ne'er before seen such a beautiful face—
So sylph-like a form—such symmetrical grace.
Then addressing the courtiers, who stood at each
    side,
" Her beauty would ruin a city," he cried ;
" In truth she is lovely and wondrously fair !
And, if she is willing, I solemnly swear,
That she, by whom I but just now was accursed,
Shall, of all my imperial brides, rank the first !"

In a moment a plan in her mind she revolved :—
For the tyrant she never would wed she resolved,—
Concealing her feelings, she hastily cried,
" Since your majesty wishes to make me your bride,
First grant me three things ; their fulfilment ensures
My heart's dearest wish—after that, I am yours."
The Emperor felt very pleased and elate,
And bade the young girl at once fearlessly state
These three things ; she had only to say what they
     were
'Twould gratify *him*, could he gratify *her*.

The maiden, emboldened, arose from her knees,
And exclaimed, " The three things that I wish for
     are these ;—
First build me a bridge over which I may ride,
From hence to the Wall, ten *li* long, ten *li* wide ;
Next build for my husband a tomb ten *li* square ;
And lastly your highness must sacrifice there,
In mourning robes clad ;—thus my mind will be
     eased
And, buried with honour, his manes appeased,
If your majesty grant these three things you will
     earn
My life-long devotion and love in return.

The Emperor smiled, and his breast glowed with
     pride ;
" Your wishes," cried he, " shall be soon gratified

Such trifles as these, they are nothing at all;
What is building a tomb, or a bridge, to the Wall?"
The imperial mandate soon spread far and wide,
And workmen assembled from every side;
They worked with such diligence, history says,
That the bridge and the tomb were complete in three
     days.

This diligence made the imperial heart glad,
And he instantly ordered the court to be clad
In white mourning robes; and he next orders gave
To march in procession to *Wan-hsi-liang's* grave;
He, placing himself, with *Mêng Chêng*, at its head,
In a chariot of gold forth the long *cortége* led,
When they came to the tomb, the Emperor bade
Them all kneel, while himself the due sacrifice made.
All obeyed his commands; next the Emperor flung
Himself on his knees by the side of *Mêng Chêng*.

While prostrated thus, the Emperor thought,
" 'Tis her beautiful face all this magic has wrought;
She is fair, but till now it has never been said,
In history either I never have read,
Of a monarch's e'er paying so heavy a price
As I have for *Mêng Chêng* in this sacrifice,
I, an Emperor, worship the ghost of a slave,
And pour an oblation of wine on his grave!"

All present in silence the spirit adored;
The monarch then rose and an offering poured

7

On the grave—three full cups of imperial wine;
This done, " Now," thought he, " the fair *Měng Chěng*
    is mine.
" Her grace, on my reign will increased lustre shed."
On reaching the bridge, when returning, he said,
" Fair maiden, my promise at length is fulfilled,
I now await yours; and to-night I have willed,
In the palace our nuptials shall be solemnized
With due pomp and show. I've already apprised
My ladies and eunuchs, and bade them prepare
Apartments befitting my queen of the fair."

———

" What!" cried the girl, " think you that I
    Could ever with a tyrant wed?
Think you that rank and power could buy
    My love from him who now lies dead?
By your harsh orders torn from me,
Slain by your cursed tyranny.

" No! I but fooled you to obtain
    A worthy burial for him!
You thought by that my love to gain,
    And gratify your latest whim.
Stuffed with conceit you dared presume
To think of conquest at *his* tomb!

" Your rank and wealth I utterly despise!
    Your presence fills my heart with fear and dread!
Your face and form are hateful to my eyes!
    I loathe the very ground on which you tread!

MENG CHENG'S JOURNEY TO THE GREAT WALL.

The air I breathe near you is odious!
I leave you now to join my husband—thus!"

As she spoke, the brave girl from the chariot stept,
With a loud cry of triumph the parapet cleared,
Plunging into the river as onward it swept,
And her corse 'neath an arch of the bridge disappeared.*

'Twas so sudden, it seemed like a horrible dream;
Both monarch and courtiers stood looking aghast,
Gazing helplessly in to the broad flowing stream,
As its deep turgid waters rushed mournfully past.

Thus the faithful *Mêng Chêng*, maiden, widow, and
wife,
To prove her devotion e'en death did not dread;
For the sake of her first love she gave up her life;
She was true to him living, she joined him when
dead.

---

* Many have it that the girl collected the bones of her
husband together, and, with them in her arms, plunged
into the river. She was canonized as the "River Goddess,"
and a temple is dedicated to her at a place called Kou-hsi
口 西. The tower which fell, revealing the bones of her
husband, has repeatedly been rebuilt, but has invariably
fallen again. The story goes that it never can be built
without toppling down again as soon as it is finished.

7 *

The song of *Mêng Chêng* and her journey is finished;
Since she sought her husband long ages have passed,
Yet the halo around her shines on undiminished,
And *will* shine so long as this empire shall last.

And so long as our race love to hear tales of glory,
And the bosom throbs high when a brave deed is
    sung,
So long will the breast swell at hearing her story,
And the tear fall in pity for faithful *Mêng Chêng*.

THE ILLNESS, DEATH, AND FUNERAL OBSEQUIES OF MR. LOCUST,

WITH A SLIGHT ACCOUNT OF THE BATTLE AT HIS GRAVE.

Mr. Locust reclined on the branch of a tree,
As bad as a locust could possibly be:
(All knew he had been for a long time asthmatic;
The cold autumn winds too had made him rheumatic;—
Now locusts know well, for experience has taught 'em,
If not well wrapped up they take cold in the autumn.)
   He'd a cold on his chest,
   And at night couldn't rest;
   What with coughing and sneezing,
   Hawking, spitting and wheezing,—
He got feverish too; this went on until
He became, as they term it, alarmingly ill.

He would cough till near choked; his breathing was
    thick,
And his groans would have softened the hide of a tick.*

In this sad dilemma he called for his wife,
Who sprang to his side, frightened out of her life.
Cried he, " Send at once for the doctor, my dear,
'Tis certain as fate if he isn't soon here
I shall make you a widow;—there, don't go and cry,
For I haven't quite made up my mind yet to die.
Don't be so absurd as to give way to grief,
It's too soon yet; but come here, and straighten this leaf,
For I don't feel quite easy ; now prop up my head ;
And please bear in mind that I'm not yet quite dead.
         Now go—come back—stay !
         My dear wife, come, I say,
         Tell me, what's your idea
         Of Cicada—has he a,
         In his pharmacopœia
A cure for my asthma—a-a-panacea—
A something to rid me of this dreadful pain
And manage to make me a locust again ? "
         The wife cried, " My dear,
         Let us hope for the best;
         When the doctor comes here,
         He'll prescribe for your chest,
And very soon put you all right, never fear ; "—
But she thought in her own mind, " His end 's drawing
    near."

---

* *Lit.* Dog-bean (狗 豆).

Mrs. L., in the soft chirp a sick bed requires,
Called her son, whose long legs seemed hung upon wires;
Bade him hop off *instanter* to fetch the physician,
And not play by the way, or be long on his mission.
  " Skip to Dr. Cicada,
   And beg him to aid a
Sick person, your father, and say I'm afraid a
Crisis approaches, and I've thought it but proper
To send for him here to meet Dr. Grasshopper,*
Talk over the case and try what can be done
For your father, for two heads are better than one."
Young Locust sprang off, and tho' not yet " in wings,"
He hopped, skipped, and jumped with tremendous long
  springs,
And soon reached the doctor's; who, hearing the news,
Packed up such few drugs he might chance want to use;
Then gravely hopped off, with Young Locust as guide,
And soon found himself at the patient's leaf-side,
When he drew from his pocket two shagreen receptacles—
One containing his physic, the other his spectacles.

   His specs he adjusted,
   And said that he trusted
His patient was not quite so bad as was stated;
   But his lower jaw dropped;
   He suddenly stopped;

---

 * Dr. Grasshopper, probably by an oversight of the author's, is not shown or mentioned as consulting with Dr. Cicada on the case afterwards.

And his long face, ere long, longer grew—elongated :
>
> For he saw in a moment,
>
> Neither physic nor foment

Could ever take *that* cold from poor Locust's chest ;

> Prescribe what he would,
>
> It could do him no good,

But these cogitations he kept in his breast.

> (If colds are neglected,
>
> It can't be expected

They can *always* be *cured*, but, there ; patients know best.)

He began, " Ha ! Yes ! Hum ! My dear sir, I beg

You'll show me your tongue. Now stretch out your hind
leg."

> The patient obeyed,
>
> And the doctor then laid

His hand—or rather his feeler—he put

> On Locust's right wrist,
>
> Not the wrist of the fist,

But his feeler he put on the wrist of his foot.

" Hum ! 'Tis merely a cold. I will write a prescription

I've found very soothing in every description

Of cold or catarrh—I invariably give it.

> 'Tis syrup of squills,
>
> With two opium pills,

If you take it you'll soon be ' as right as a trivet.' "

He said this to cheer him, and although 'twas untrue,

'Tis a thing that all doctors, in his place, would do.

He then mixed up a dose, and in taking his leave,
Called the matron aside and bade her not grieve;
    " She musn't be scared,
    But be fully prepared;
For, alas! of her poor husband's life he despaired.
How long he would last he'd not venture to say;
It might be a week; he might pop off to-day.
He was called in too late; he had done what he could;
As for physic or doctors they could now do no good,
For when it once came to the push—die he would."
He concluded, "His life, ma'am, is not worth a fig;
I'll stake my existence he'll soon 'hop the twig.'"

The widow prospective her tears quickly dried,
And hastened once more to her husband's leaf-side;
She administered the dose, though she didn't expect
It would be of much use, yet she watched the effect.

After taking the physic the patient was seized
With a strong fit of coughing; he then three times
    sneezed;
Soon he felt Death's cold hand on the tip of his nose:
Stretched his legs slowly out, gasped, and turned up his
    toes.

The news of his death soon far and near spread;
Friends came—some to show their respect for the dead;
Others, merely to see what there was to be made
In what may be called their "legitimate trade."

Mr. Grig, the undertaker,
Was Locust's coffin-maker ;
He soon made a natty box, into which they placed the
    dead ;
The draper, Mr. White Moth,
Supplied the mourning cloth :
Mr. Spider set to work and built the funeral shed.*

Of course, those who bore Locust's family name,
When they heard of his death, one and all quickly came ;
These probably numbered a hundred or more ;
At their head was his favourite nephew *Kuo-kuo 'r.*†
Dragon Fly was requested to act as M.C. ;
Mr. Snail‡ was deputed to pour out the tea ;
Greasy Locust,§ as usual, was *chef-de-cuisine*,
And served out the soup in an acorn tureen.
(In the foregoing couplet the translator took
A slight liberty—*chef-de-cuisine* should be " cook : "
Instead of " served *out*," the word *should* be " served *up;*"
For " acorn *tureen*," read " a large acorn *cup;*"
" Cook " is not so euphonious as " *chef-de-cuisine*,"
Nor is " large acorn cup " as " an acorn tureen."

---

  * At Chinese funerals a mat-shed is built over the
courtyard in which the coffin is placed ; it is unlucky if
the sun or moon shine on the coffin.

  † 蟈蟈兒. A species of locust.

  ‡ 水牛, " water buffalo," is the common name for
snail.

  § 油渾螞蚱.

See what euphony does; just to put *two* lines straight,
The translator, alas! is compelled to write *eight*.)

Mr. Skipjack* and Mr. Grasshopper were waiters,
To attend to the wants of the guests and spectators;
These were, Mr. Louse, Messieurs Fowl and Wood-
    Louse;†
(Mr. Snag, and the latter, each brought his own house.)
Miss Lady-bird‡ came, with Ant, Earwig and Bug;
Caterpillar, with Grub, Maggot, Weevil and Slug.
Mr. Mantis was there, so was young Little Mite;
Mr. Worm crawled in late, with him came Mr. Blight.
Messieurs Fly, (House, Gad, Fire, Bluebottle and Horse,)
Made themselves busy on each side the corse.
Mr. Tick, though an invalid, managed to come;
All knew Mr. Gnat's whereabouts by his hum.
Messieurs Cockroach and Beetle appeared clad in mail;
Mr. Scorpion came, with his sting in his tail.
The Centipede§ family came in full force;
Poor Buzzing Musquito, he cried himself hoarse.

---

* 賣油的 "Oil-seller," and 跑堂兒的 "Hall-
runner," or, "waiter," are the terms most commonly used
for "skip-jack."
† 濕濕虫 "Damp-damp-insect."
‡ 愛飄 "Love-to-whirl."
§ Among the centipedes mentioned is one called 錢串
"Cash-strings." This sort is very plentiful in most
houses, and is perfectly harmless.

White, yellow and painted, there mustered a score
Of the Butterflies—with them they brought 'Hei lao
　　po'r,*
Whose son, Master Moth, though reputed a scamp,
For this once neglected his old flame Miss Lamp.
Fighting Cricket—he chaunted the prayers for the nonce,
And a full choir of Crickets chirped every response.
Cantharides† came with Cockchafer and Flea ;
The music was led by our friend Humble Bee.
Assisted by Honey Bee, Wasp and Old Drone—
As the latter was bass he played the trombone.
Young Grig played the flute and the talented Hornet
Brought out some melodious strains on the cornet ;
The cymbals were beaten by Master Gold Bell ;‡
Gnat played on the trumpet remarkably well.
Death-Watch beat the drum with an incessant knock ;
Most excellent time too was kept by the Clock.§

The procession was formed, and of course, at its head
Went Young Locust,‖ who carried the "board" of the
　　dead.

---

    *黑老婆兒 "Dame Black," a large black kind of
moth.
    †班毛 or 班貓.
    ‡金鐘兒 a species of cricket, much admired by
Chinese for the pleasant bell-like sound it makes with its
wings.
    § English local name for " beetle."
    ‖ It is the duty of a son to go in front of his deceased
parent's funeral procession, carrying his 靈牌, "Spirit
tablet," or " board " as is here translated.

There were four hoarse Cicadas to keep the road clear,
And sixty-four Locusts to carry the bier;
Eighty Scorpions, two and two, went on before,
And the funeral paraphernalia bore;
The Fireflies and Glowworms a brilliant light showed—
For 'twas dark ere the *cortége* set out on their road.
The widow, in white, followed next to the bier;
Swarms of friends and relations then brought up the
    rear.
When they started the M.C. some brief orders gave,
And, conducted by Lizard, they soon reached the grave,—
For Mole-Cricket and Beetle had already made
A nice roomy grave with their pickaxe and spade.

As they stood round the grave, the deep silence was broke
By an unearthly sound—the Bull-Frog's hoarse croak;
(His hoarseness was probably brought on by damp)—
This sound made a good many mourners decamp.
Alas! they well knew what that dread sound implied,
'Twas the cry of their foe; soon, their mouths open wide,
Came squadrons of Frogs, with Bull Frog at their head,
Their martial array struck the mourners with dread.
Some, who had wings, were soon seen in full flight,
But all who had stings were determined to fight.

On bounded the Frogs, they were met by the Bees,
But nothing could stay them, they gobbled up these:

Re-forming again, they rushed on at full speed,
Charging madly the troops led by Old Centipede;*
The carnage was dreadful, cut, parry, and thrust.
And many a brave Centipede bit the dust.
They next put the Hornets and Wasps to the rout;
Dead bodies on all sides were scattered about.

The Scorpions bravely defended the corse,
And three times repulsed the ferocious Frog Horse;
Each Scorpion making good use of his tail—
Their courage, alas! was of little avail;
Every charge of the Frogs in their ranks left great gaps;
One by one they went down some rapacious Frog's chaps.
Overpowered at length, they all turned tail and fled,
And left on the ground many wounded and dead;
These the Frogs ate at leisure, and soon swallowed all,
Including the bier, corpse, coffin and pall;
Then retired to their pool, which they quickly regained,
And once more o'er the battle-field deep silence reigned.
Not a vestige, when dawn first appeared in the east,
Remained of the Funeral, Battle, or Feast.

---

* 老 蜈 蚣. Probably the " royal centipede " is here meant.

THE INSECTS' PROPHECY,

OR

THE DEATH OF KING PA.*

—————

Closely pressed by his foes in the darkness of night,
Faint and weary King *Pa* still continued his flight;
His troops had been scattered and slain in the strife,
He, alone, and a fugitive, fled for his life.

He reached the Black River and paused there to rest,
Looking hopelessly out on its dark turgid breast;
When, chancing to cast round his eyes, he espied
A boat safely moored to a bush near his side.

———————————

* Han Hsin, 韓信 the general by whom the troops of
King *Pa*, 霸王, were defeated, is said previously to have
written the prophecy—with honey—probably anticipating
such result as the above from the well-known superstition
of his opponent. The insects were naturally attracted to
the stone by the honey, and unconsciously formed with

He leaped in the boat and, propelled by an oar,
The frail bark was soon far away from the shore;
Here at least he was safe, for his foes would not dream
He was,—thanks to the boat,—far away down the
     stream.

He felt safe when once out on the river's broad face,
He could drift off unseen, leaving no sign or trace;
Being weary and sleepy he lay down and slept,
While noiselessly on with the tide the boat swept.

As if led there by fate—dawn scarcely had broke,
When the boat neared an island, King *Pa* too awoke;—
Gazed round for a moment, then seizing an oar,
He rapidly guided the boat to the shore.

He leaped on the bank, no mortal was near,—
But what made King *Pa's* ruddy face blanch with fear;
On a large rock before him these words caught his
     eye;—
" At the mouth of the Black River King *Pa* will die! "

---

their bodies the living words of the prophecy 覇 王 烏 江
喪, *Pa-wang wu-chiang-sang* (by rights the character *k'ou*
口 " mouth " should follow after *chiang*), as seen by King
Pa, which playing on his superstitious fears induced him
to commit suicide. Some say he did so by cutting his
throat.

     It is said that King *Pa* was so strong that he could
blow the tiles off the roof of a house (力 吹 房 上 瓦).

THE INSECTS PROPHECY.

This sight filled the heart of the monarch with fear :
" 'Tis strange ! so, 'tis prophesied I shall die here !
What hand could have written this strange prophecy
' At the mouth of the Black River King *Pa* will die !' "

" What mystery's this ? "   He drew near to view ;
But the words stood out bolder the nearer he drew :
" What demon such strange looking words could con-
    trive ?
" They move too—by Heaven ! all the words are alive !"

Yes, like a thick crust, on the rock's face there swarmed
Myriads and myriads of insects, which formed
With their *bodies* the words of this wierd prophecy—
" At the mouth of the Black River King *Pa* will die !"

" What ! do even the meanest of insects unite
My sentence of death with their *bodies* to write ?
I *must* be accursed then, when *they* prophesy
' At the mouth of the Black River King *Pa* will die ?' "

The air seemed alive with the horrible words—
They were borne on the breeze, they were sung by the
    birds—
The stream gently moaned them—the trees seemed to
    sigh—
" At the mouth of the Black River King *Pa* will die !"

8

There they were, on all sides—on the hill—on the
    plain—
Impressed on his heart—burnt into his brain ;—
On each bush and stone—on the earth—in the sky—
" At the mouth of the Black River King *Pa* will die !"

" 'Tis writ I shall die here—*they*'ve prophesied so—
But no menial weapon shall strike my death blow."
He drew forth his sword, plunged it into his side—
At the mouth of the Black River thus King *Pa* died.*

---

    * History gives quite a different version of the death of
Pa Wang: "Closely pursued by the troops of *Han-hsin* he
reached the banks of the Black River, where a boat was in
waiting to convey him over to the opposite side where he
would be safe among his own people. The boat-keeper,
named *Ting-chang,* 亭 長, entreated him to cross over and
escape ; but *Pa Wang* resolutely refused to do so, averring
that he could not face the elders of his native place after
his defeat. Turning to the few followers who were with
him, he told them a thousand pieces of gold were offered
for his head by *Han-hsin,* and bade them take it to him
and receive the reward. He then drew his sword, and in
their presence cut his own throat."

    Pa Wang was thirty-one years of age when he died. He
was born in the fifteenth year of the reign of *Ch'in Shih-
'huang,* 秦 始 皇, and died in the twelfth month of the fifth
year of *Liu-pang* 劉 邦 of the Han dynasty.

THE RAT AND THE CAT IN HADES.

Thrice the drum beats, and thrice the golden bell,
Through " Spirit Land," booms forth its awful knell ;
Thrice cracks the whip,*—its sharp resounding thong
Strikes terror in the breasts of that vast throng.
Hushed is the court, no sound the stillness breaks ;
Each " spirit judge " his seat in silence takes ;

---

* When the Emperor goes to sacrifice, an official, carrying a whip, stands on each side of the palace gate. It is the duty of these officials to " crack " their whips. This description of whip is called P'i-mang, 皮 蟒 (leather snake). Its handle is about eighteen inches, and the lash upwards of six feet in length. When the whip is " cracked " it sounds like the report of a pistol, and can only be used for the noise it makes, adding—the Chinese

8 *

A constant stream of spirits come and go,
Some looking joyous, some o'erwhelmed with woe.
On a high throne, where every eye can see,
The King of Hades* sits in majesty ;
Around him throng his ministers of state ;
Kneeling, before him, trembling spirits wait
To hear the words which tell them of their fate.

Then spoke Yen Wang :—" Since the Almighty Power
Struck heaven and earth from Chaos, till this hour,
He destined *Me* His behests to fulfil ;—
My acts are but the workings of *His* Will.
Having *His* power to help, *His* skill to guide,
All earthly crimes I equably decide.
No mortal man can e'er ' Dark Heaven ' deceive,
His puny skill the subtlest arts may weave.
Poor human skill or wisdom, what are they ?
Man's darkest plots to *Him* are bright as day.
To serve *Him* He conferred that power on me,
And *I* also man's inmost heart can see ;

---

say—to the impressiveness or majesty of the occasion.
When Manchu Bannermen commit themselves, they are
flogged on the buttocks or legs with whips ; twenty-seven
lashes only can be given at one sentence, though another
twenty-seven can be administered immediately after, or,
indeed, any amount of twenty-sevens, each twenty-seven
being separately ordered.
    * Yen Wang.

Ere yet a crime is *thought*, that thought I read,
And know the consequences of the *deed*.
The wish that *must* precede the fatal blow,
I, ere 'tis expressed in thought, already know.
Sooner or later all on earth must be
Brought hither to receive their doom from me ;
Both good and bad before me must be tried—
According to their merits I'll decide."

    While Yen Wang was speaking
    A scratching and squeaking
Was heard at the door ; and he cried, " Who is that ? "
    A voice sharp and clear,
    Piercing every ear,
Shrilly squeaked, " Let me in, I'm the ghost of a rat !
    Grant me admission ;
    I bring a petition ;
I've suffered injustice, and hither have come.
    Let me in, I implore,
    Or I'll scratch down the door,
And nibble a hole through the head of the drum ! "

" Admit the rat," exclaimed the King ; " the meanest
    thing that crawls
Shall have its share of justice meted out within these
    halls."
The Rat now entered shyly and advanced towards Yen
    Wang,
Throwing suspicious glances right and left upon the
    throng.

Then kneeling at his feet, it squeaked, " Your gracious
    Majesty,
Deign but to read this paper, and you will plainly see
That I've been foully "—" Yes, I know," the monarch
    quickly said ;
Then opening the paper, its contents he loudly read.

      " Complainant deponeth,
      And publicly owneth,
He's the ghost of what once was a peaceable rat :
      He further declareth,
      And solemnly sweareth,
That his *body* was slain by a murderous cat."

" He is seven years of age, and during that time,
He avers he has never committed a crime ;
But has lived in his hole at the foot of a wall,
Never poking his nose out till after night fall,
Then only to nibble a few grains of rice,
Pick a bone, or anything else he saw nice ;
(As for stealing, *en passant*, he'd scorn such a vice).
He admits that he *pilfered*, but never once *stole*,—
This fact may be proved by inspecting his hole.

" What complainant has suffered exceedeth belief,
Through wrongfully being put down as a thief ;
When he 's been chased as one, to his hole he has fled,
And many a time has gone hungry to bed.
He has often, e'en though he felt hunger's keen pangs,
Stopped at home, for fear of the cat's keener fangs.

When he *did* quit his hole, it was always at night,
And by stealth—even then too, he trembled with
  fright.

" Near to complainant's hole there lived a cat,
Of savage mien ; well-clothed, well-fed, and fat ;
When pleased, she'd purr and curl her long moustache,
When in a rage, her tail she'd fiercely lash.

" Her eyes were like two bells—like knives her claws ;
Long sharp white teeth protruded from her jaws ;
She frightened him, for when she mewed or swore,
To *him* it sounded like the tiger's roar.

" One night complainant went out for a stroll,
But scarcely had he left his peaceful hole,
When suddenly the cat with furious bound,
Sprang on, and hurled complainant to the ground.

" He vainly strove,—at length he grew so weak,
He could do nothing else but faintly squeak ;
While she, the cat, each moment fiercer grew,
And bit complainant's back-bone through and through.

" Then dashed him up and down in savage play,
And clawed and mouthed him, till at last he lay
A lifeless heap, bleeding at every pore ;
Exhausted nature could endure no more.

"Head, legs, and ribs, nay, every bone she crunched ;
From nose to tail as savagely she munched
His palpitating flesh ;—bone, hair and hide
Found a mausoleum in her inside.

" Complainant had no animosity
Against the cat, and therefore fails to see
Why she, to gratify a murderous whim,
Should, unprovoked, make sausage-meat of him.

" The law says, ' life for life.'   Does not a rat
Enjoy life just as keenly as a cat ?*
'Tis not for base revenge complainant seeks ;
'Tis but for justice that he loudly squeaks,
And humbly begs your Majesty will send
A warrant off at once to apprehend
The Cat, and bring her hither to be tried,
And bear what punishment you may decide.
Complainant squeaks for justice on the Cat
For murdering
        Your Unoffending,
               RAT."

---

   * The idea conveyed in this sentence is not unlike
Shylock's, " Hath not a Jew eyes," etc.

When Yen Wang had read
The petition, he said,
" Come hither, Horse Face—you too, Bullock's Head ;*
You'll both of you go to the house of the Cat,
Bring her here on a warrant for murdering Rat."

Bullock's Head and Horse Face
At once left the place,
And went on their way at a deuce of a pace ;
For a whirlwind they strode,
Which both *sprite*fully rode,
Till at length they alighted at Pussy's abode.

The unconscious Cat
By the kitchen fire sat ;
Her hind legs and breast she was cosily warming ;
She purred with enjoyment
At her pleasant employment,
For she was then busy her toilet performing.

Her enjoyment was brief,
It was soon turned to grief ;

---

   * 馬 面 and 牛 頭, attendants at the court of Yen
Wang ; apparently, from their duties, runners or lictors.

Bullock's Head and Horse Face now entered and bound
her,
> Put a chain round her neck,
> And at once hurried back
With the Cat in her *déshabille** just as they found her.

Once in the hall, the scene that met her view
Made Pussy cock her back and spit and mew;
Her downy fur erewhile so smooth and bright,
Now, in her fear, stood rigidly upright.
Of rats and mice she had encountered hosts,
She feared not them, but, ah! she feared their ghosts;
And here were ghosts of every size and shade,
Enough to make the stoutest feel afraid.
Rats, mice, pigs, sheep, cows, horses, cats and dogs,
Birds, beasts, and fish, snakes, lizards, toads, and frogs,
While every species of the human race
Were represented largely in this place.

On one side of the hall the wicked spirits stood,
The other side was occupied by the spirits of the good;
The Cat looked on in wonder at such a constant flow
Of spirits passing in and out and hurrying to and fro.

Yet everything was noiseless, no banging to of doors:
No whispering; no shuffling sounds upon those sound-
less floors;

---

* As will be seen in the sequel, 'twas the *spirit* of the
Cat only that was taken, not the body, which the text leads
one to infer.

Though not a word was spoken, the scenes which
    transpired could
Not only be distinctly seen, but fully understood.

Those who crossed the "golden bridge" straightway to
    heaven went ;
Those with "horns and feathers" to hell forthwith
    were sent ;
Those who on earth in wantonness had taken human
    lives
For everlasting had to climb up mountains made of
    knives.

Incendiaries wallowed in a lake of burning fire ;
Hacked and hewn to pieces were the slanderer and liar;
The wasteful and improvident, who made improper use
Of wealth, were now with "Iron Dogs" and "Copper
    Snakes" turned loose.

Boiled in wine were those who were partial to the cup;
Cheats were, by two devils, in a mortar pounded up ;
Swindlers had their hearts torn out ; but the hateful
    brute
Who cursed his parents, had to tear his tongue out by
    the root.

The Cat looked on in silent wonder,
        And frightened mien
        Upon this scene ;
When suddenly a noise like thunder

Through the hall reverberated ;
  Her hair with fright
  Stood bolt upright;
Her stiffened tail with fear vibrated ;
Her smellers bristled up with horror :
" What were they now preparing for her ? "

There was more yet in store,
  For an opening door,
Whose hinges apparently hadn't been greased,
  Made a harsh grating sound—
  And the Cat too jump'd round—
She was more and more with astonishment seized.

Soon the whole room
  Was enveloped in gloom,
For black clouds entered and rapidly spread
  Like a ghostly pall
  At the top of the hall ;—
These were spirits of clouds which had long been **dead.**

Then there arose a withering blast :
The Cat shrivelled up with cold and fear,
As the ghost of a gust of wind swept past
And chilled with his presence the atmosphere.

Puss was cold from her nose
To the tips of her toes,
And her teeth they chattered like dominoes,
Or the rattling of dice,—
She appeared to breathe ice,
And the blood in her veins seemed to icicles froze.

Bullock's Head and Horse Face now guarded the door,
Hasty Foot* too assisted, with two devils more.
One of the spirits now opened the case,
Which the Cat listened to with a serious face.

When complainant's attorney his statement had read,
The Cat pulled out hers, and respectfully said,
As she modestly handed it up to Yen Wang,
"Read it, Sire, you will see who's right or who's
    wrong."
Yen Wang took the paper without more ado,
And read, without pausing, the whole statement
    through.

'Twas worded thus : "Defendant is a cat—
(Perhaps 'tis not necessary to mention that,
As all in this, or any other place,
Must be familiar with her form and face.)

---

* 急 脚, another of Yen Wang's lictors or attendants.

" Defendant's duty is to do her best
To rid the world of vermin which infest
The homes of rich and poor—excepting those
Who have *us* there to drive away their foes.

" As for her private life, defendant swears
'Twas virtuous :—she daily said her prayers.*
She stayed at home, shunning the wicked wiles
Of lewd male cats who'd tempt her on the tiles.

" Defendant need not say rats are a curse ;
They pilfer all they can, and what is worse,
They've no regard for all the housewife's toil—
What they can't eat or take away, they spoil.

" They nibble edicts, for they laugh at law ;
Books of all kinds in wantonness they gnaw ;
Their notions of religion are so lax
E'en at the altar's foot they leave their tracks.

" In kitchens great disturbance they create,
Hopping from pan to cup, from dish to plate ;
'Midst pots and kettles they kick up a clatter—
The food that's in them recklessly they scatter.

---

* When a cat purrs, it is generally spoken of as "saying
its prayers " 念 佛 (Reciting the O-mi-to-fo).

" Now in a box or cupboard they bite holes;
Now in the ground they're burrowing like moles;
Now in a drawer; now beneath the bed;
Anon they gallop madly overhead.

" Now from a basket they abstract the meat;
Now in a plate of rice they wipe their feet;
Now dip a filthy nose in some choice dish,
Or in a bowl of soup a long tail swish.*

" Matrons and cooks might grind their teeth with rage;
Exterminating war might swear to wage;
Buy poison—spread it carefully on meat—
The rats would come and sniff—they wouldn't eat.

" 'Traps' and ' Brick-crushers '† near their holes were
      put;
As for the rats they wouldn't budge a foot—
They were too artful—plainly saw the *ruse*—
The dantiest bait was not a bit of use.

" They might perhaps stretch out a head and neck;
And just peep round—but quickly drew it back;
The rats were far too knowing to be caught
By any trap that ever yet was bought.

---

* Vulg. for switch.
† A brick arranged at the entrance of a rat-hole in such
a manner that the slightest touch will cause it to fall on
the rat and crush it.

" Defendant's mistress long had borne their pranks ;
At length, determining to thin their ranks
By hook or crook, she, as a last resource,
Sent for defendant, and she went, of course.

" She was well fed—nought was too good to give
    her ;—
Nice chicken bones, meat, fish, and bullock's liver,
And other tit-bits, given on the sly,
Which here defendant need not specify.

" Defendant's mistress—one and all, in fact,
Treated her kindly, and their every act
Showed for her welfare such solicitude,
As must ensure her lasting gratitude.

" The younger ladies made so much of her,
Her life was one continual state of purr ;
Their gentle hands have oft defendant fed,
Their laps have often been defendant's bed.

" Defendant fought and skirmished night and day ;
The rats she could not catch she scared away ;
All left the house, save one—*this* little beast—
Who kept her hunting him a month at least.

" One night she caught him, and without remorse,
Defendant made of him a lifeless corse ;
This, in her hate, she munched up to a pulp,
And, though 'twas nauseous, swallowed at a gulp.

" Complainant's cup of crime was not yet filled—
No sooner had the wretched thief been killed,
Than his accursed, unhallowed ghost must needs
Come hither and complain of *her* misdeeds.

" This if not promptly and severely checked,
Will make cats timid, and their tasks neglect.
Defendant, Sire, looks up with confidence :
She did her duty—that is her sole defence."

When Yen Wang had read the defendant's reply,
He foamed at the mouth, fire flashed from his eye ;
He cried, " You infernal old thief of a rat,
How dare you come hither reporting the Cat ?

" 'Tis lucky yours isn't a capital crime
Or I'd skin you!—I'll let you off lightly this time ;
You shall therefore be banished—but that's not the
    worst—
Drag him forth, and give him a sound whipping first ! "

On hearing his sentence, the Rat slily sneaked
To the foot of the throne, where he plaintively
    squeaked,
" Is this just ? Is a rat's life then counted as nought ?
Dark Heaven ! to what a dilemma I'm brought !

9

"I've been foully slain by defendant, in sport,
And then, when I bring up my case to this court,
To obtain satisfaction,—the Cat gets off free,
And again does the punishment fall upon *me*.

"Oh, Sire!" (here the Rat kept on bumping his head)
"Had I, like the Cat there, with dainties been fed,
I'd not have been caught, Sire, I pledge you my word,
By the sharpest old mouser that ever yet purred.

"Think you, Sire, I'd have ventured amongst cats and
    traps,
For the sake of their nasty old leavings and scraps?
I assure you I'd never have stirred from my hole,
For only when tempted by hunger, I stole.

"Nature made me a thief;—I hadn't a voice
In making myself;—I had therefore no choice
But to pilfer, whene'er I by hunger was driven,—
(Some are much better off, for *their* food is given.)

"Whatever has breath *must* have something to eat;
Life *must* be supported with grain, fish, or meat."—
"Stop a bit," interrupted the Cat in her turn,
"Since you must eat, like others, your food you should
    earn;
(It seems that's a 'wrinkle' you yet have to learn.)"

"Oh!" argued the Rat; "then, according to you,
Birds, beasts, and reptiles, earn their living too?—
Were it not that they gained it by rapine and theft,
There would shortly be devilish few of them left."

"Pooh, pooh!" mewed the Cat, "How obtuse you must
    be!
Wherever there's *you* there must always be *me*;
Men hunt beasts and reptiles, by that you perceive,
Men, like *cats*, are sent hither to catch those who
    thieve."

Squeaked the Rat, "One would fancy, to hear you thus
    mew,
That the world was created expressly for you!
(I confess that I hold quite a different view.)
Because there's a *sun* in the sky, why not swear
That the moon and the stars had no right to be there?"

Yen Wang struck the table and bade them both cease,
Nor stop there and argue disturbing his peace;
"Do you know where you are? Do you think I'll
    allow
At the foot of my throne such an unseemly row?

"Birds, beasts, and fishes, all things that have life,
To keep it, must wage a perpetual strife;
All strive to get food in the best way they can,
But they mustn't, by any means, prey upon man.

9 *

"As it is amongst *you*, so 'tis also with men ;
They prey on each other with sword, tongue, or pen,—
The strong on the weak, the great on the small
The rich on the poor, and the king upon all.

"Flog the Rat!   Let him into the river* be hurled!
Take the ghost of the Cat quickly back to the world.
From henceforth let rats and descendants of rats,
Be food for all cats and descendants of cats."

———

The Resuscitation of the Cat.

Meanwhile Pussy's *body*, while this scene occurred,
Lay prone on the stove and never once stirred ;
Her form was supine, her legs were outstretched—
She lay as she fell when her spirit was fetched.

Dame Wang came in soon after and saw her faithful
     mouser
To all appearance dead—she started back aghast ;
She felt her heart, 'twas warm ; she tried in vain to
     rouse her ;
Disheartened with her efforts, she gave it up at last.

———

* Actually, the "Forbidden River" 禁 河, wherever
that may be.

She gave vent to her sorrow in bitter lamentations ;
She wrung her hands in anguish at seeing stark and
    stiff
The poor Cat's corse, unheeding her endearing appella-
    tions ;—
She'd give the world to hear her purr or give the
    faintest sniff.

" You were, when last I saw you, as playful as a kitten,
So full of life and health scarcely half-an-hour ago ;
Now you're lying here, by death's hand rudely smitten;
I never thought to find you thus, poor puss ! Ai ya !
    Ai yo !

" I was always in a tremble, for fear some dog should
    worry
Or otherwise maltreat you, when you went into the
    lane ;
If I missed you for a minute, not a house but I was in
    it,—
I never gave up searching till I had you safe again."

Would nothing save her ? Dame Wang heaved a sigh ;
    To save her poor cat's life she'd grudge no labour ;
She'd call her spirit back, at least she'd try—
    So off she went to some kind-hearted neighbour
To borrow " paper cash ; "—for this ingredient
In case of life or death is deemed expedient.

    *   *   *   *   *

The dame now proceeded to sacrifice :—
In a bowl of clean water she flung some rice ;
She burnt in a dust-pan the paper cash ;
Three joss-sticks also were burnt to an ash.

The branch of a peach tree she placed at the side
Of the corpse of the Cat; then thrice she cried,
"Five Gods! Five Gods! my prayers don't spurn,
But soon my poor cat's spirit return."

"Oh! spare my cat! Her life restore!
And priests my gratitude shall pour
Before your shrines in constant prayer.
Five Gods! Five Gods! my poor cat spare!"

Her prayer being ended, she closed-to the door;
The water and rice she poured out on the floor ;
The bowl she placed over the corpse of the Cat,—
This she struck with her thimble three times, rat, tat,
    tat.

As her thimble each time hit the bowl a sharp whack,
The dame at that moment called out "Puss, come
    back!"
Her lips had scarce uttered the last plaintive word,
When the old lady's prayers were not only heard,
But answered as well ;—this is how it occurred :—

Just at this time Bullock's Head and Horse Face
Were bringing the Cat's spirit back to the place;
This they put in the corpse, and, unseen by the dame,
Departed at once in the same way they came.

The spirit no sooner had entered the Cat,
Than she stretched out her legs, sneezed, sniffed,
    winked, and spat;
And ended by quietly sitting upright,
To, it's needless to say, the old lady's delight,

Who faced the north-west, and as she did so,
With closed hands recited her O-mi-to-fo!
Then thanked heaven and earth, and the five gods as
    well,
For sending her cat's spirit safe back from hell.

THE WRY-NECKED TREE.

At the foot of Prospect Hill stands an old distorted tree;
  'Neath its shade have often walked the Mings in all
    their pride.
It saw the first and last of that mighty dynasty,
  For 'twas planted by *Yung-lo*, and on it *Ch'ung-chên*
    died.

Though leafless and distorted now, it was not always so;
  Its foliage was luxuriant, its trunk was tall and
    straight;
Now, 'tis called the Wry-necked Tree, for two hundred
    years ago
  The old tree bent its haughty head beneath a monarch's
    weight.

Two hundred years ago
  What an awful stir
    There must have been
  'Neath the Wry-necked Fir,
    When at dawn was seen
The corse of *Ch'ung-chên*
In the bright morning sun,
As it swayed on a branch to and fro.

Yes, it is he!
  The corse that swings
On the Wry-necked Tree
  Is the last of the Mings.

His race, alas! is run;
  No more will he
    Sway with his single Will,
  Or govern the destiny,
Of "all beneath the sun."
    At the foot of Prospect Hill,
  The last of a dynasty,
A king—the "Solitary One"—
  Hangs on the Wry-necked Tree.

It must have been
  A strange sight
To have seen
  At morning light
The corse of a king
From the old tree swing.

Every one near
  Shuddered with awe,
And paled with fear
  At the sight they saw;
The white ghastly face
Of the last of his race
Seemed to look down,
  From the old tree's bough,
On the group with a frown
  And a lowering brow.
Lower it gently—the corse that swings
On the Wry-necked Tree is the last of the Mings.

Who knows what was said
At the last parting scene
Of *Ch'ung-chên* and his queen,*
Ere barefoot he fled
In the dead of the night,
Nor stayed in his flight
  Till he reached the old tree
On which he now swings?
  Fulfilling his destiny;
Last of the Mings.
  Untold in History 's
His parting with her;
  Shrouded in mystery 's
His death on the fir.

---

* Tradition says that the Empress committed suicide, and the princess, her daughter, was slain by the Emperor to prevent her falling into the hands of the rebels.

The last hours of *Ch'ung-chên*
Are known only to *One*.

When lowered to the ground,
   In his breast
A paper was found,
   Thus addressed :
" To *Li-tzu-ch'êng*,
   When I am found dead,
On the fir tree hung,
   Let this paper be read.
Those our last wishes are written by *Us*."
The paper was opened ; the writing ran thus :

" Imperial brother, *Li-tzu-ch'êng*, I most devoutly
   pray
That if there *must* be slaughter, you'll *all* my
   courtiers slay ;
But, oh! my loyal subjects, my black-haired
   people spare,
On no account slay them—grant this my earnest
   prayer."*

---

* The actual words of the paper as given in the song
are :—

拜上拜上多拜上　拜上皇兄李自成　要殺殺我文合武　千萬別殺好黎民

What shall be done
        With the tree
Which hung *Ch'ung-chên?*
        Which dared
Bear such imperial fruit?
        Shall it be spared,
Or grubbed up by the root,
        And die with the dynasty?

The tree that has gained
        Such unholy renown
Shall not be cut down;
        Let the culprit be chained.*
It thus shall remain
        Till the end of time,
Bound with a chain
        For its awful crime.

The rebel *Li-tzu-ch'êng* lived in the palace eighteen days.
He had sufficient respect for the deceased Emperor to place
him in his coffin and sacrifice to him.

* *Shun-chih*, the first Emperor of the Ch'ing dynasty,
ordered the tree to be chained. He also granted permission to inter the body of the Emperor in the family
tomb.

When the old fir tree
    Shall be freed from its thrall,
The Ch'ing dynasty
    Will totter and fall.*
May such a catastrophe never occur
As removing the chain from the Wry-necked Fir.

---

* It is believed that should the tree be ever unchained, great calamity would befal the reigning dynasty. To this day the tree remains chained, but it has almost fallen to the ground.

DAME KUO'S VISIT TO HSI-TING FAIR.

Dame Kuo was a matron, close verging on fifty,
Reputed to be, too, remarkably thrifty;
She had money galore, but knew how to enjoy it—
Her thriftiness being how best to employ it
So as to get all the good she could *out* of it—
And she fully succeeded—there can't be a *doubt* of it.

The buxom Dame Kuo
Made her mind up to go
To the fair which is held once a year at Hsi-ting ;—*
A place of resort
For religion or sport—
A temple, in fact, fifteen *li* from Peking.

---

* 西頂. This is a temple, in which a fair is held every year from the 1st to the 15th of the fourth moon.

Dame Kuo mounted her cart,
Gave the signal to start,
After seeing her hand-maidens carefully put
Into carts standing near,
Which now followed in rear ;—
She'd a guard too, comprising both mounted and
foot.

These numbered a score :—
Some behind, some before ;
While some to the shafts of the carts lent their aid,*
Lest the ladies inside
Should feel terrified.
Thus they formed, altogether, a grand cavalcade.

What giggling and tittering took place within those
carts !
What sheep's-eyes thrown at passer's by—more deadly far
than darts ;—
Inflicting wounds incurable on many throbbing hearts.
What a constant munching too there was of apples, cakes,
and tarts !

---

* It is common to see servants running by the side of
a cart with one hand on a shaft—probably assisting themselves by this process, rather than to be at hand lest the
occupant of the cart should call them.

Dame Kuo had got a "sipping flask,"* but as she rode
    alone,
How many sips she *did* take is not accurately known;
But that she *had* required a sip her beaming features
    showed;
For when she reached the fair with benevolence they
    glowed.
En passant, too, inside her cart, a hamper† had been
    stowed
Lest she should want substantial creature-comforts on
    the road.

When they came to the temple a servitor ran
To inform the old Abbot—and he, worthy man,
Bade tea be served up in the flick of a fan—
    With the best that his larder could boast.
He invited the matron to enter and rest;
And proud at receiving so welcome a guest—
(For she was a "patron"—and one of his best)
    He at once commenced duty as host.

---

   * 呃壺兒. This is made of pewter, and has a
"sipper" screwed on, similar in use and shape to those on
babies' sucking bottles. These "sipping flasks" can be
slung over the shoulders on a journey.

   † 菜斗兒. Made of wicker work, and not much
unlike a very large "sandwich case." These can also be
slung over the shoulder.

Having finished her tea, the buxom Dame Kuo
Made a sign to her maids she was ready to go.
Then she rose from the table, declared she had
    done ;—
She would stroll round the fair now, and look at the
    fun.

Depositing a *douceur* in the Abbot's willing hand,
She said, in words the old priest couldn't fail to
    understand :—
"When the fair is finished, you must come and hunt
    us up;
You'll always find a welcome, and a bed, a plate, and
    cup."

Dame Kuo made her way through the thick of the
    fair,
And old as she was, not a young lady there
Enjoyed herself more, or felt greater delight,
Than she did at every queer sound or strange sight.

    Buying and selling,
    Screaming and yelling ;
"By your leave! Stand aside! Can't you see where
    you 're going ? "
    Roaring and shouting,
    Ranting and spouting,
Cymbal banging, flute squeaking, and long-trumpet
    blowing.

Gonging and drumming,
Fiddling and strumming,
Interspersed with a good deal of squalling and bawling.
Hawking and talking ;
The girl slack-rope walking—
" How nicely she does it ! "—Ai, ya ! she is falling ! "

Cursing and swearing,
Peeping and staring ;—
" This, ma'am, is the stall, if you want a nice fairing.
Here are all sorts of toys,
For good little boys,—
Red-string, flowers, and knicknacks, for young ladies'
wearing.

" Here are mouth-pieces made
From the purest of jade,
And pipes that will make bad tobacco smoke pleasant.
Thimbles, scissors, and knives,
For industrious wives ;—
Make a choice from my wares—there's no time like the
present."

Losing and winning,
Laughing and grinning,
Humming-top spinning ;—on dry land boats rowing ;
Horses a-neighing,
Donkeys a-braying,
Begging priests praying ;—stilt-walking, stone-throwing.

Whirligging* and swinging,
Story-telling, bell-ringing.
A drummer is singing, at the same time is plying
Three sticks; two he beats with,
And performs sundry feats with;
While the third one in mid-air is constantly flying.

Snuffing and smoking,
Jesting and joking,
Or saying smart things, which set people laughing.
Bear-dancing; folks rushing,
And each other crushing,
To hear merry-andrews their audience chaffing.

What a hubbub and din;
"Just going to begin!"
What changing of money! what taking and giving!
At the door people paying;
Within, actors playing:
And puppets which look just as if they were living.

Clod-hoppers swarming
To see rats performing,
Or peep-shows, with gay scenes which constantly vary.
"For three cash may be seen
A girl—aged sixteen,
With the legs of a horse and the face of a fairy!"

---

* A whirligig—similar to those used in English fairs,
is called 傘 輪 子 "Umbrella Wheel."

10 *

Female tumblers—athletes,
Performing strange feats;
Quack doctors, rogues, thieves, and beggars, are numerous;
Some, pity exciting;
Some, squabbling and fighting:—
Here are scenes of all sorts, grave, gay, sad, or humorous.

Dame Kuo having seen all the sights of the fair,
And drank as much tea as her stomach could bear;—
Besides buying fairings for each of her maids,
Such as hair-pins and ear-rings, tags, tassels, and braids,
Climbed into her cart and returned to Peking,
Well pleased with her trip to the fair at Hsi-ting.

INVERTED FACTS.

1st Month.

In the first month we keep up the Dragon-Boat Feast;*
The sun, at this time, always sets in the east;
Temples are never built facing the south;†
(How glibly a crammer slips out of one's mouth!)

A stout man is one with no flesh on his bones;
Singing is sighing commingled with groans.
Fasting and praying, or doing good deeds,
If indulged in, to all sorts of wickedness leads.

---

* This festival really occurs on the fifth day of the fifth month.
† Exactly the reverse.

You cannot make oil out of hempseeds or beans ;
The beggar 's a person who lives on his means;
A rich man is one who works hard for his bread,—
At daybreak we usually go off to bed.

Tinder 's a difficult thing to ignite :
Dogs love to bask in the sunshine at night :
Charcoal 's a fruit which makes capital pies ;
Truth is language consisting entirely of lies.

2ND MONTH.

In the second month all vegetation decays ;
What people term censure, is nothing but praise.
At midnight the sun is high up in the sky,
And the swallows to northern climes rapidly fly.

Rivers and streams always flow to the west :*
Bad things are good, but the worst is the best.
Brimstone 's a dainty—it 's best when it 's boiled ;
Hinges, to work well, should never be oiled.

A soldier's chief duty is drawing his pay;
In battle, 'tis chiefly in running away ;
His diet consists of pure calabash soup ;—
One man is a regiment, two form a troop.

---

* Chinese believe that all rivers *must* flow eastward.

All ladies should bow, and men fold their arms ;
A beldame's a maiden of unsurpassed charms.
Those only have doctors, who are anxious to die ;
Those only tell truth, who infernally lie.

3RD MONTH.

In the third month the warmth makes the green snow-
    flakes freeze ;
And cotton is gathered from mulberry trees.
Those who are fasting eat sugar with meat ;
A *gourmand* is one who's too lazy to eat.

When one has invited a friend home to dine,
'Tis an insult to ask him to take bread or wine.
When a person gets tipsy it's always on tea ;
The favourite perch of a mule, is a tree.

On the top of a chair two stout bearers ride,
And carry the horse, who sits down inside.
In beating a gong, you a feather employ ;
A man is a woman, a girl is a boy.

When one is merry, the eyes stream with tears ;
When one is sad, the face smiling appears.
Anger is shown by a round beaming face ;
A waddling or lop-sided movement is grace.

4TH MONTH.

In the fourth month the autumn wind bitterly blows ;
When the cock lays an egg, the hen loudly crows.
The sun and the moon always rise in the west;
Love-sickness is caused by a pain in the chest.

The fish is a bird ; when it's angry it sings ;
'It builds in a tree, and its legs are all wings.
The horse is a quadruped having eight legs ;
It burrows a hole—some one else lays its eggs.

The tiger 's an insect, it lives in the sea,
Its chief occupation is gathering tea.
A scholar 's a person unable to read ;
A dunce is a man very clever indeed.

The hair on a bald head is long, coarse, and thick ;
An athlete is a cripple who walks with a stick.
A dummy is one who can fluently speak ;
A straight-forward person 's considered a sneak.

5TH MONTH.

In the fifth month the weather is growing more cool ;
The fool is a wise man, the wise man a fool.
A duck's egg is shaped like a gourd-calabash,—*
It takes twice to lay it, and costs fifty cash.

---

* Something like ♂.

Ten piculs are not near so heavy as one;
A misanthrope's one who appreciates fun.
At eighty, a small child commences to walk,—
In a few hundred years he'll be able to talk.

A tippler is one who abominates drink;
'Tis charming to hear a dog yelp "pen-and-ink."
Fish, in a stream, love to stroll on its banks;
On receipt of a flogging, one murmurs one's thanks.

A coward is one who's a stranger to fear;
The tiger slinks off, at the roar of the deer.
At the sight of a mouse, the poor cat runs away;
A candle is commonly lit at mid-day.

6TH MONTH.

In the sixth month the fields are all covered with ice,—
Now is the season for transplanting rice.
At this time, too, spiders fall victims to flies,
Who hang up their webs on to hooks in the skies.

In writing, the most proper thing one can use
Is a catty of lard, and a pair of straw shoes.
Clever people are plentiful—not so are fools;
Illiterate men are inspectors of schools.

A mat-shed is better by far than a house;
An elephant 's nearly as big as a louse.
The lichee is long, and as sharp as an awl;
Sugar-cane, all well know, is as bitter as gall.

'Tis said honey 's sour, and vinegar 's sweet;
Going opposite ways, is described as " to meet.''
Killing a man 's not considered a crime,—
So long as you kill him but *once at a time.*

7TH MONTH.

In the seventh month the weather is bracing and clear,
Old and young wear gauze clothing to hail the new year.
How delighted folks are on receiving abuse !
Money or food is of no earthly use.

Heaven always protects an undutiful son,
But 'twill punish severely a dutiful one.
'Tis a pleasure to see a girl smoking a pipe;
The chief of the 'Han-lin 's a seller of tripe.

Those who make money, in general, lose;
Taking all as they come, is to pick and to choose.
All kinds of pastry are called " butcher's meat;"
The soles of the hands are the calves of the feet.

To die of old age is called " premature death,"
This is caused by a rush of superfluous breath.
The cypress and fir are the trees that fear cold,—
They are hardy, and therefore don't live to be old.

8TH MONTH.

The eighth month is spring, it comes once in three years;
How bright, and how beautiful, nature appears!
The willows how red! The peach-blossoms how green!
Those pigs in the gutter, too, are they not clean?

Consumption is only a sign one is strong,
Those who have it severely are sure to live long.
Blind persons are those who pretend they can't see;
Quite lately, an old man was slain by a flea.

If a woman is dark, we exclaim, " Oh, how fair!"
To modestly cast down the eyes is " to stare."
When a person is nude, he is " tastefully dressed."
A dying injunction 's considered a " jest."

A child should be flogged, if he does what is right;
Good deeds are oftenest done out of spite.
Black is white—so is red; the sunshine is shade;
A hoe is a rake, but a broom is a spade.

9TH MONTH.

In the ninth month the apricot blossoms look blue,
And vie with the pear in its bright sable hue;
The slender elm clings to the stout pumpkin tree;
Grapes grow on the boughs of the green yellow pea.

The frogs warble forth their melodious notes,
In a gush of sweet music—as if they 'd sore throats.
The cats bark in concert; and a dunghill close by
Wafts its fragrance far up in the dark crimson sky.

Figs are dug out of mines and to good uses put,
Boors sell them for firewood, at so much a foot.
One is always athirst after taking a drink;
The odour of flowers is called a vile stink.

Last night 'twas so hot that it actually snowed;
A gutter is merely a broad level road.
'Tis pleasant to see all the vessels sail by,
When the bed of a mountain is swoll'n till it 's dry.

10TH MONTH.

In the tenth month the weather is getting quite warm;
The centipedes now are beginning to swarm;
The snakes and the scorpions fly through the air,
In pursuit of such birds as they find grazing there.

The sparrow transfixes the hawk with his beak;
Deafness, is being unable to speak.
The butcher was killed by a blood-thirsty lamb,
For daring to look while he suckled his dam.

When rain falls in torrents, the ground is quite dry;
A girl that's too forward is said to be "shy."
The blue clouds are often concealed by the sun;
A job, when complete, is considered undone.

Elation at what we have done, is "regret;"
When one shivers with cold, that is called a "muck-
    sweat";
A cast in the eye is a capital crime,—
'Tis death by the law to cast both at one time.

11TH MONTH.

In the eleventh month the weather is dreadfully hot,
And people put on all the clothing they've got.
If you wish to make tea, that is easily done,
Boil your water at night in the shade of the sun.

A long row of willows is called an oak tree;
The elbow 's a joint at the bend of the knee.
When a raven is singing he purses his lips;
A bright sunny day is a total eclipse.

In cold winter weather the heat is intense ;
Reality 's only a name for pretence.
If a man dies of hunger they say that he 's gorged ;
Chain armour is woven, silk clothing is forged.

Men walk on their hands—these they put into shoes ;
To travel by land, is called, " taking a cruise."
A cat is a dog, and young kittens are pups ;
Plates are teapots and kettles, but chopsticks are cups.

12TH MONTH.

In the twelfth month 'tis hot, for Midsummer is come ;
The peach trees break down with the apple and plum ;
The calabash trees are all loaded with fruits,
Which the rustics, with ladders, dig up from their roots.

Men who shun women are styled " wicked rakes."
There is nothing a gambler dislikes more than stakes ;
Don't say, "you speak true—" that 's an improper term,
And a person will turn if trod on by a worm.

When a coffin is dead, he is placed in a corse ;
A camel 's a cow, but a bear is a horse.
If you speak of the present, you say, " by-and-bye ;"
When you *know* one speaks truth, then be sure 'tis a lie.

The last month is finished, so, too, is my song;
If you look, you 'll perceive it is just twelve months long.
It contains many facts, which some folks may deem
To be falsehoods,—but all things are *not* what they seem.

THE BEATER'S SONG,

OR

TING-LANG'S SEARCH FOR HIS FATHER.

Hail New Year!
Welcome New Year!
How bright the lamps in the streets appear!
Ting-lang had been
Through the streets and seen
The crowds and lights to hail the New Year!
Peaceful Year! Year of peace!
May our blessings and wealth increase!

The boy went home when the three drums beat *
And flung himself at his mother's feet;

---

* Midnight.

Where, hiding his face in her lap, he kept
Fast hold of her hand as he loudly wept.
    Peaceful Year! Year of peace!
When will the tears of the poor boy cease!

    "Tell me, darling—tell me why
    You thus bitterly sob and cry.
    Into my bosom pour your grief;
    Who but a mother can give relief?"
    Peaceful Year! Year of peace!
Soon shall the tears of my darling cease!

"Mother, whenever I'm in the street,
I'm jeered by every boy I meet;
They say I've no father—have got no name;
That I'm only a child of sin and shame.
Can it be true, mother, what they say;—
That I am a bastard—a waif—a stray—
A floating weed—a toadstool sprung
From the vilest of places—a heap of dung?
That you, mother, you, I so much revere,
Were—? let me breathe the vile word in your ear,—
But I *knew*, mother darling, *that* was untrue,
For the angels are not more pure than you!"

The mother had listened with drooping head,
To all that her weeping son had said;
When he'd finished, her head she proudly raised
And lovingly into her boy's eyes gazed.

11

" Ne'er heed, my child, what the street-boys say,
For you are no more base born than they.
It harms you not if they look with scorn,
For you, my son, were in wedlock born.

Then she told to her child all her history,
Which till now had to him been a mystery.
Of her childhood's days ; of the time she wed ;
Of the happy life as a bride she led,
Till his father, one fatal day, was sent,
For another's crime, into banishment.
She told him where he 'd been sent, and how
He had changed his name from *Tu* to *Kao*.

He now had been gone twelve weary years ;
And the mother described her hopes and fears,
In the long, long years she 'd had to wait,
Without one line to tell his fate ;—
Of the many and bitter tears she 'd shed—
Of her lonesome life, and her constant dread
Lest his father died 'ere his name was freed
From the stain of committing a fearful deed.

" Mother, I'm but a boy ;
But can I here remain,
And lead a life of joy,
While you live one of pain ?

Ah, let me go in quest
Of him you hold so dear!
Nor will I ever rest,
But wander far and near,
Till I have found him, cleared his name,
And brought him hither free from blame.

" Yes, mother, I must go,
For while I linger here,
A witness of your woe,
Each moment seems a year.
If strength and years I lack,
My love will bear me through;
And soon I'll bring him back
To home, to love, and you.
In such a cause I must succeed;
Your blessing now is all I need."

The mother was loth
From her brave boy to part;
" What, if I lose both!"
Thus whispered her heart.
Yet her grief she concealed
In her innermost breast;
She could not but yield
To his urgent request.

"Go, my son; seek your father, but quickly return;
Bring him safe, and my undying gratitude earn.

11' *

But your zeal, my brave darling, has made you
    forget
That you don't know your father—you've not seen
    him yet."

Thus saying, three proofs from her bosom she drew,
Exclaiming, "I transfer these tokens to you;
Of each of these three parting keep-sakes you see,
He kept one half and gave one to me.

" See, this is my half (the other he took)
Of the mirror we broke at our parting, and look,
Here's half of the comb at my wedding I wore,
And this is my part of the 'kerchief we tore.

" How many long years in my bosom they've lain,
When will they with *his* halves be united again!
Whoever these three parting tokens can pair,
Is your father, my husband—we both his name bear."

The half of the mirror, the 'kerchief, and comb
    The boy safely placed in his breast;
For at dawn the next morn he'd quit his loved home,
    And his courage be put to the test.

Why dwell on the sad parting scene which took
    place;
'Twas made up of hopes, doubts, and fears;
He would ever remember her pale anxious face,
    She would pray for his safety with tears.

Mid sobbing and tears and heart-rending sighs,
  They at length bade each other adieu ;
She watched her boy's progress with tear-blinded
  eyes,
  Till his lithe form was hid from her view.

     Day after day,
     On his weary way,
The brave lad journeyed without delay ;
     Resting at night,
     But at morning light
Hurrying on with all his might ;
And as he went on his way he pressed
The parting tokens he had in his breast.

     Lower and lower
     The lad's small store
Sank, till he hadn't a farthing more ;
     With his cash all spent,
     Still he onward went,
Begging his way from door to door.
The roadside at night for his lonely bed,
And a stone to pillow his weary head.

For days and weeks on trudged *Ting-lang* ;
To his joy, at last, he neared Hsiang-yang ;
'Twas here that his father had been sent
Twelve years before into banishment.

With brimming eyes on the distant town
The young lad gazed—then kneeling down,
He prayed that his father still might live—
And that *he* might his father freedom give.

Tired and faint, the lad that night
Slept on the ground in the broad moonlight,
And in his sleep he dreamt he heard
His parent's history word for word,
Arranged in verse to a simple air—
The echo, it seemed, of his evening prayer.
The tale was breathed in his thirsty ear
In a voice so musical, soft, and clear,
That at once the words and the melody
Sank deep in the dreamer's memory;
The words, and the music—every note—
The boy, in his dream, had learnt by rote.
Then a choir of voices, blythe as birds,
Warbled in concert the following words :—

          "*Ting-lang!   Ting-lang!*
       When you reach Hsiang-yang,
   Go to the place where the builders throng.
          Where the builders throng,
            Sing the 'Beater's Song,'
   And you'll find your father, my brave *Ting-lang.*"

The melodious voices died away,
Still *Ting-lang* on the roadside lay

Murmuring over and over again,
In his sleep, the words of the last refrain :—
    " Sing the 'Beater's Song,'
      When you reach Hsiang-yang,
And you'll find your father, my brave *Ting-lang*."

The lad slept on till daylight broke,
When, refreshed with rest and sleep, he woke,
Got up, and with hope his young face glowed,
As he once more trudged o'er the dusty road,
The song and tune engraved on his mind,
And certain his father with these to find.
Soon he entered the city gate,
Resolving near it awhile to wait :
But who cau imagine his heartfelt joy
When a man accosted him thus :—" My boy !
If you want employment, come home with me ;
And you've only to name what your wages will be,
If you can lead in the Beater's Song."
(My dream will come true now, thought *Ting-lang*.)

      The overjoyed lad
      Was only too glad
At the prospect of finding his father he had ;
      And at once replied,
      He would like to be tried,
And he trusted the man would be satisfied.

They reached the spot, and raised above the throng,
The lad was placed, to sing the Beater's song ;
He felt his tokens, breathed an earnest prayer,
Paused for a moment, then the simple air
He trilled forth in a clear and plaintive strain,
The workmen's voices chaunting the refrain.

THE BEATER'S SONG.

" I'm a poor little boy, all the way from Peking;
     Beaters, Ho ! Ho ! Ho ! Ho ! Hai !*
In search of my father I've come here to sing ;
     Beaters, Ho ! etc.
I bade mother good-bye on the first of the year ;
     Beaters, Ho ! etc.
And, on foot, I have travelled from Peking to here.
     Beaters, Ho ! etc.

" When I left home the ground was all covered with
  snow ;
     Beaters, Ho ! etc.
That sometimes I hardly knew whither to go ;
     Beaters, Ho ! etc.
Spring came with its flowers and warmth-giving sun ;
     Beaters, Ho ! etc.
'Tis now the sixth moon, and my journey is done.
     Beaters, Ho ! etc.

---

  * The mallet, or rammer, falls at the word Hai ! which
is a sound not dissimilar to that made by a pavior in
England.

" What hunger and thirst I endured in that time !
    Beaters, Ho! etc.
What rivers to cross ! what high mountains to climb !
    Beaters, Ho! etc.
'Gainst hardships untold I had not strength to cope ;
    Beaters, Ho! etc.
Were it not that my bosom was buoyed up with hope ;
    Beaters, Ho ! etc.

" Though a beggar, I come of a good family ;
    Beaters, Ho! etc.
My father had taken his second degree ;
    Beaters, Ho! etc.
And hoped, like his ancestors, honour to earn ;
    Beaters, Ho! etc.
Which he could transmit to his children in turn.
    Beaters, Ho! etc.

" My father's bright dreams were soon rudely dispelled ;
    Beaters, Ho! etc.
For a villain the face of my mother beheld ;
    Beaters, Ho! etc.
And struck by her charms, to obtain her resolved ;
    Beaters, Ho! etc.
E'en though it his own death or ruin involved.
    Beaters, Ho! etc.

" To further his schemes, the base traitor *Yen* ;
             Beaters, Ho ! etc.
Found constant employ for my poor father's pen ;
             Beaters, Ho ! etc.
And cloaking his purpose, contrived to pretend ;
             Beaters, Ho ! etc.
To be to my father his most faithful friend.
             Beaters, Ho ! etc.

" My father one night went to *Yen's* house to sup ;
             Beaters, Ho ! etc.
When well warmed with wine, the wretch drugged his
    cup ;
             Beaters, Ho ! etc.
And while he was senseless, *Yen* murdered a slave ;
             Beaters, Ho ! etc.
And then charged my father with the blow that he gave ;
             Beaters, Ho ! etc.

" He was dragged off to prison, the torture applied ;
             Beaters, Ho ! etc.
But the crime for a long time my father denied ;
             Beaters, Ho ! etc.
Till worn out with anguish at last he confessed ;
             Beaters, Ho ! etc.
Yen's crime, was by torture, thus wrung from his breast.
             Beaters, Ho ! etc.

" *Yen* now sought my mother and offered his aid ;
Beaters, Ho ! etc.
But she firmly refused all the offers he made ;
Beaters, Ho ! etc.
Then he dared speak of love, but she laughed him to
scorn ;
Beaters, Ho ! etc.
For *she* loved the sire of her child yet unborn.
Beaters, Ho ! etc.

" He then ventured her bright almond eyes to admire ;
Beaters, Ho ! etc.
This aroused all my poor mother's virtuous ire ;
Beaters, Ho ! etc.
' You admire my bright eyes ! You shall do so no more !'
Beaters, Ho ! etc.
She exclaimed, as an eye from its socket she tore.
Beaters, Ho ! etc.

" My father was banished from Peking for life ;
Beaters, Ho ! etc.
Sad was the parting 'twixt husband and wife ;
Beaters, Ho ! etc.
By the unfeeling guards they asunder were torn ;
Beaters, Ho ! etc.
In the midst of my mother's distress I was born.
Beaters, Ho ! etc.

" My father has now been away twelve long years ;
Beaters, Ho ! etc.
My mother has mourned him in sorrow and tears ;
Beaters, Ho ! etc.
Lapse of time, which so often produces relief ;
Beaters, Ho ! etc.
But gave an additional sting to her grief.
Beaters, Ho ! etc.

" I grew up, and boy though I was, I could see ;
Beaters, Ho ! etc.
That the task to console her devolved upon me ;
Beaters, Ho ! etc.
So I left home and her on the first of the year ;
Beaters, Ho ! etc.
And in search of my father have begged my way here.
Beaters, Ho ! etc.

" I'll sing for my father wherever I go ;
Beaters, Ho ! etc.
And I *know* I shall find him—my heart tells me so ;
Beaters, Ho ! etc.
He *must* hear my voice, for I never will rest ;
Beaters, Ho ! etc.
Till *he* pairs the tokens I have in my breast.
Beaters, Ho ! etc.

" I shall soon hear his voice, and see his dear face ;
    Beaters, Ho ! etc.
For he's here in this city, perhaps in this place;
    Beaters, Ho ! etc.
His real name is *Tu*, but the name he bears now;
    Beaters, Ho ! etc.
He assumed to conceal his disgrace,—it is *Kao !* "

    Scarce had he sung that name, when, lo !
        Without a warning sound ;
    A servant struck the boy a blow,
        Which felled him to the ground.

    The poor boy stunned and bruised,
        An effort made to rise ;
    His fair young face with blood suffused,
        Tears streaming from his eyes.

    Too weak to stand alone;
        Blinded with blood and tears,
    He sank down with a groan,
        But now a voice he hears—

Exclaiming in accents reproachful, yet mild,
" How dare you, base villain ! thus strike the poor child !
You, a man too ! alas ! have you no sense of shame ?
Does your manhood consist in nought else but the name ?

" Wipe the blood from his face ; bring him hither to me ;
He's not a mere stroller—I plainly can see ; "
The servant replied not, but hung down his head,
And the boy to the matron he speedily led.

It chanced that the matron while busy within,
Had heard the sweet voice of young *Ting-lang* begin,
And had run to the window, where, hid by a screen,
She had looked down below on the bustling scene.

She was struck by the boy's extreme youth and his grace,
His soft plaintive voice, and his beautiful face ;
She had followed his tale through the whole of the song,
And her woman's heart pitied poor little *Ting-lang*.

But when the boy mentioned his father's false name,
Her eyes flashed with anger, her face flushed with shame;
'Twas *her* husband's name, there was   shame   in   the
      thought !
She, too, was the wife of the father he sought.

But, ah ! when she saw the boy felled to the ground,
With not one to aid him amongst those around ;
Her good feelings speedily smothered the bad,
She would now do her utmost to comfort the lad.

The dame spoke kindly to little *Ting-lang*,
   Who modestly stood there with bended head ;
" Sing me the words of the Beater's Song ;—
   I'd like to hear them once more," she said.
" Sing them again for me, line for line,
I would see if *your* tale tallies with mine."

As the boy commenced singing his story once more,
His father, unknown to him, entered the door,
Sat down, little thinking the boy he heard sing,
Was his son by the wife he had left in Peking.

The story went on—each line *Ting-lang* sang
Conveyed to the father's proud heart a fresh pang;
'Twas his own tale he heard, and the boy was his son;
But how could he rectify what had been done?

The dame read his guilt in his tale-telling face;
She was angry and grieved at his being so base;
She was angry to think she had been thus deceived;
When she thought of his first wife and child she felt
    grieved.

Her eyes flashed with scorn, shame mantled her brow,
When the boy sung *his* father's—*her* husband's name,
    Kao;
And pointing her hand to her husband, exclaimed,
" There, child, is your father, the *Kao* you just named."

" 'Tis false," said the father; " your wits must have
    fled;
Till I married this lady I never was wed;
Your whole tale's a tissue of lies, I declare!
I've no wife or children at Peking, I swear!

" If I am your father, what day did I leave?
How old am I now?—Don't attempt to deceive.
When and where were you born? and what tokens have
    you
To prove what you just now asserted, is true?"

To these queries young *Ting-lang* with candour replied:
And the father, expressing himself satisfied,
The sanguine boy, to set all doubts at rest,
The three parting tokens now took from his breast.

When his father saw these, he exclaimed with a groan,
" Yes, they are her proofs;" he then drew forth his own;
Comb, mirror, and 'kerchief—the whole of the three,
Were found, when compared, to exactly agree.

Thus the boy found a father, the father a son,
But the father remorsefully thought of *that one*
He had left at Peking, all these years in suspense;
And *this one!* what plea could he urge in defence?

" Alas!" cried the father, " my crime has been great,
And no words of mine can my guilt palliate;
But remember, my son, I was banished for life,
What hope had I then of rejoining my wife!

" At that time I thought I in exile should die,
That *she* for my fate would not fruitlessly sigh ;
I thought not a moment she'd constant remain,
But wed with another, a home to obtain.

" She indeed has drank deeply of grief's bitter cup ;
What trouble, unaided, in bringing you up !
Should I see her, her kindness I'll amply repay ;
My son, she shall never want more, from this day."

    Ting-lang the starting tear suppressed,
      And to his father said,
    " How coldly are your words expressed,—
      Are all your feelings dead ?

    " Why use such words as ' if ' or ' should ? '
      You're wealthy now and free ;
    Had you the heart and will, you could
      Go back to her with me.

    " On whom, save you, should she depend?
      Ah ! did you know but how
    She's struggled on, without one friend,
      Since you left home till now !

    " My mother has but rags to wear,
      You're clothed in silks and furs ;
    You dine upon the choicest fare,
      The coarsest food is *hers.*

" My mother occupies a shed,
    You live in luxury ;
A straw mat is her only bed,
    You sleep luxuriously."

The matron was shocked at her husband's duplicity,
    Carried on for eleven years with an unruffled brow ;
She had spent all this time in domestic felicity,
    And never suspected his guilt until now.

All her feelings and sympathies now were enlisted
    On behalf of her rival, her husband's first wife ;
She would be as a sister, and nobly insisted
    She should stay with them here for the rest of her life.

While speaking, the wife saw her husband grow pale ;—
Human help at this time was of little avail ;
He gasped as if wishing to speak—with a groan,
He staggered, and then to the earth he fell prone.

Ting-lang and the wife saw him fall, with dismay ;
It looked like a judgment—be that as it may ;
They endeavoured the unconscious man to revive,
Impatiently waiting till help should arrive.

The leech came at length, and with serious face,
Pronounced it paralysis ; said that the case
Could never be cured—'twas beyond human power :
The patient, though living, was dead from that hour.

The blow was severe to his wife and his son ;
His *second* wife thought the best thing to be done
Was to send for his *first* wife to come to Hsiang-yang,
To live there together with her and *Ting-lang*.

She therefore despatched a man off to Peking,
With a letter, some funds, and directions to bring
The wife there at once ; but the servant returned
With the news that both money and offer were spurned.

In a letter, however, the first wife had sent,
After thanking the second, she said her intent
Was to wait till her husband recovered his health
And returned to Peking ;—she was careless of wealth.

Time passed till the lad reached the age of sixteen,
When he took his degree ; his ambition had been
To excel in his studies : his first being gained,
He studied, and at seventeen his second obtained.

His father, meanwhile, all these years had been ill—
His sickness, as yet, had defied human skill,
Till a poor priest, whose life had been spotless and pure,
Tried *his*, and effected a permanent cure.

Both father and son to Peking now returned,
The boy proud of showing the honours he'd earned,—
Proud of his father's accession to wealth,
But prouder of seeing him once more in health.

12 *

At length, son, husband, and wife once more met;*
But, alas! all their trials were not over yet;
The meeting was glad, but their union was brief,—
'Twas changed in a moment to wailing and grief.

While recounting the sufferings each had gone through,
Some ruffians rushed in, and without more ado,
Seized the husband 'gainst whom the old charge had been
    laid;
He was bound, and again to prison conveyed.

The mother and son wept in silence awhile;
At last the brave lad raised his head with a smile,
Exclaiming, "Dear Mother, trust all now to me,
And I'll strive night and day till I set father free."

Ting-lang worked, for he had a great purpose in view—
The 'Han lin degree; and he very well knew
He must win to save *him*, a much higher aim
Than merely the honour of gaining a name.

He was first on the list, and what words can express
His delight when he heard of his brilliant success!
Three hundred and sixty succeeded that day,
But he, out of all, the chief prize bore away.

---

* From the time of *Ting-lang* and his father quitting
Hsiang-yang, the second wife drops out of the narrative
altogether; her kindness evidently receiving no gratitude.

At Court, when the winners—the *crême de la crême**—
Were examined again, his was still the first name.
The flowers and red cross† were bestowed on *Ting-lang*,
While before him men beat thirteen strokes on the gong.‡

Soon after, young *Ting-lang* was summoned to court;
He went, placing first in his breast a report,
In which he his father's old foe had impeached,
And justice against the arch-traitor beseeched.

When at court, *Ting-lang* knelt at the foot of the throne;
Chia-ching bade him rise, in a mild, kindly tone,
And applauded his essays, on which the young man
Conceived that the time was now ripe for his plan.

---

* These number only eighteen, those first on the roll of successful competitors for the Chin-shih degree. The successful one out of this eighteen obtains the degree of Chuang-yüan, which constitutes him a member of the 'Hanlin. The victor is consequently considered the greatest scholar in the empire for that year.

† The flowers are called golden flowers, 金花, but are merely tinsel, and are not *bestowed* on the successful candidate—he buys them himself, and sticks them into his official hat. The red cross is a long strip of silk arranged in such a manner as to come over both shoulders of the wearer, and cross both on the breast and the back.

‡ At the present day the gong is carried in front of the victor (but not beaten), as are also four square red flags and a red umbrella. The victor parades the streets with all these paraphernalia.

He held up his report, which the Emperor took;
Ere he'd read many words there was wrath in his look.
" Base dog ! " he exclaimed, " 'tis a villainous plot !
How dare you impeach the best servant I've got ! "

Then he flung the offending report to the ground;
But a gust caught the paper, and whirling it round,
Placed it down on a table which stood by his side,—
All wondering what this proceeding implied.

The Emperor's wrath was more great than before,
He dashed down the paper again on the floor;
But again by a gust was it caught up and whirled
Round and round, and again on the table was hurled.

" This is too much ! " the monarch exclaimed, with a
    frown,
And a third time the paper he fiercely dashed down;
But again by the wind, as before, 'twas conveyed
Through the air, and again on the table was laid.

The courtiers trembled; the Emperor said,
" Dark Heaven has decreed the report should be read !
I therefore obey ; "—he then took the report,
Which he read in a loud voice before the whole Court.

His eyes were now opened; he now saw that *Yen*
Was a traitor to him, and the vilest of men :
Perpetrated by him (these were certified facts)
Were over a hundred tyrannical acts.

Yen was seized and degraded—of his clothing was
    stripped,
By the chief executioner publicly whipped ;
His estates, confiscated, to *Ting-lang* were given,
While he from the Court as a beggar was driven.

The name of his father was now free from stain ;
He was quickly released and returned home again,
Where, once more united, son, husband, and wife,
Having passed all these trials, lived happy for life.

Yen wandered the streets with bare bleeding feet,—
He was scoffed and reviled, he was hooted and beat ;
He suffered from hunger, but none dared bestow
A handful of rice on their now humbled foe.

Four days had passed thus : he was growing so weak,
Through hunger and thirst, he could now scarcely speak ;
His eyes became bloodshot, his lips parched and dry,
Strange sounds filled his ears, and he knew he must die.

Yet he still staggered on, and now feeble signs made
For help, but no hand was stretched out to his aid ;
And this man, who a short time before swelled with
     pride,
Exhausted, sank down on a dunghill and died.*

---

* Many parts of this song have been curtailed, or
omitted, as being unintelligible to the foreign reader
without very copious notes.

THE CAPTIVE MAIDEN.*

'Tis very like my home.   Yes, I can see—
As like as art can make them—facing me,
The balustrade, the gate, the massive wall,
The great pavilion, too, o'ertopping all.

---

* The Emperor *Chien-lung*, 乾龍, had a Kashgar maiden
sent to him, whom he loved very much, and who became
his favourite concubine. Lest she should too deeply mourn
her distant home, he had a tower built in the palace, called
Wang chia lou, 望家樓 (Behold home tower).   Immediately facing it, and separated from it only by the palace
wall and a road, he caused to be built the *fac-simile* of her
Kashgar home, in which he allowed the retainers who
accompanied her to dwell, so that the girl could constantly
have the prospect of her distant home before her, and
even converse with her countrywomen when she felt disposed.   One can scarcely imagine a more delicate and
touching way of showing the love he felt for the Kashgar

Within those courtyards I can now and then
Catch glimpses of some old familiar face—
A wife or daughter of those Kashgar men,
Wearing the costume of my native place.

---

girl than *Chien-lung* exhibited, though it is probable, as the song would imply, that it had an effect quite the reverse of what he intended; serving only to make her gorgeous imprisonment all the more intolerable by perpetually reminding her of that home she was never destined to behold again.

Wang-chia-lou is in the same portion of the palace in which is situated the building where the Audience took place, and may be seen by anyone passing up the Chang An Street, 長安街, as may also the 'Hui tzŭ ying fang, 回子營房 (Mahomedan's Quarters), opposite. Many of the descendants of the followers who accompanied the girl still live in or near the building, and, after this lapse of time, are undistinguishable from the Pekinese. Some of the women, however, still adhere to the peculiar Kashgar *coiffure*, which consists, among girls, of their hair being first plaited in a number of small queues, sometimes a dozen or more, and plaiting these again into one large queue, beads or pearls being tastefully disposed among it; and also wearing a round cap striped with various bright colours. Married women wear two queues, one on either side, also the striped cap.

Each male of the girl's escort was allowed three taels a month by *Chien-lung*; this amount they and their descendants continued to receive till *Tao-kuang* cut it down to one tael per month, which each male descendant receives at the present time. Being Mahomedans, when one of them dies he must be buried within twelve hours of his decease; the corpse is washed clean, wiped dry, swathed in cotton cloth and placed in a coffin, and borne

'Tis very like my home. But, oh! I miss
That other home the more I look on *this;*
I miss loved forms that made my home so dear,
Those who made home a *real* home appear.
I do not see my kindred, and I feel
The loss of them, the cruel blank they leave;
I gaze, and *try* to picture *this* as real :
Alas! the more I gaze the more I grieve.

'Tis very like my home. From yonder tower,
Breaking the stillness of the twilight hour,
In the soft accents of my native tongue,
I hear the ballads of my country sung.
But that is all, there the resemblance ends,
This only makes me grieve and crave for more;
I long for other voices, those of friends :
'Twould *then* be like the home I had before.

---

in it to the grave. The grave consists of a hole dug in
the ground to the depth of six or seven feet, with a sort
of recess scooped out in the side of the pit, of the same
length as the corpse, and high enough for a person to
kneel within (it being supposed that on the third day
after interment the corpse rises to kneel and pray). The
corpse without the coffin is then placed within the recess,
prayers are read, the grave covered in, and a hillock raised
over it similar in shape to those of England and other
Western countries.

'Tis very like my home.   But yet its walls,
Too oft and much my other home recalls ;
Filling my breast with many a vain regret,
With recollections I would fain forget :
'Twas built in kindness, yet 'tis mockery ;
It makes me pine, when *he* would have me gay ;
Why do I look?   Oh ! that my home should be
So very near, and yet so far away !

DON'T MARRY A WIDOW.

T'other day, as I found I'd a few hours to spare,
I went for a stroll, just to breathe the fresh air;
But I hadn't walked far, when in front I perceived
An old man approaching who seemed deeply grieved.

He was wringing his hands, and as nearer he drew,
I could see he was crying—and bitterly too.
An old man shedding tears is a sad sight to see—
At least, it has always appeared so to me.

I said to him, "Tell me the cause of your grief!
The mere telling often produces relief.
Are you poor? If you be, that I'll soon rectify.
Are you childless?—Pray tell me the reason you cry."

The old fellow no sooner heard what I said,
Then he gave over crying, and shaking his head,
Exclaimed :—" If you'll deign, Sir, to listen a space,
I'll relate in a few words my pitiful case.

" A short time ago,
You must know,
I had money, and houses, and land ;
Wife, daughter, and son—
Alas ! *now* I've none !
I'm filled with despair,
For of all I'm stripped bare,
As bare as the palm of your hand.

" Yes, Sir, a short time since, I had every wish in life ;
A cosy home, a boy and girl, a good and loving wife ;
I'd gardens, fields, and orchards, where grew the peach
and date—
In short, Sir, I may safely say I had a fine estate.

" I'd three mules and a donkey—for two carriages I
kept ;
The mules were stout—as for the ass, a finer never
stept.
My yard was amply stocked with pigs, and ducks and
fowls and geese—
The gobblers, they would always fetch at least five *tiao*
a piece.

Ah! I was happy then, Sir, but "—here the old man
    cried—
" In the midst of all my happiness, alas! my poor wife
    died!

" How wretched I felt on receiving this blow,
    I'll leave it to you to conceive;
I neglected all else to give way to my woe,
    And for weeks I did nothing but grieve.

" One day when my sorrow began to abate,
    A go-between came with the news
Of a widow who'd make me a capital mate—
    Just the sort she was sure I should choose.

" The widow was youthful and handsome as well,
    She was rich too, the go-between said,
And willing—but why on this painful theme dwell?
    A week after that we were wed.

" As she entered, she looked like an angel from
    heaven;—
So young, too!—the go-between said twenty-seven;
But *she* was mistaken, for I'd have sworn *then*,
Out of spite the old lady had added on ten.

" Such cherry lips ! Such pearly teeth ! Such cheeks !
    Such hair ! Such eyes !
And I, myself was master of so beautiful a prize !
She had a good big dowry, too, so everybody thought;—
This is the inventory of the things my second brought :

     " A watch-dog to bark,
     And prowl round in the dark,
     To keep thieves away ;
     A donkey to bray—
     With elongated jaw
     To e-e-e-haw !

     " Ten flat-flat-billed ducks,
     Drains and gutters to cleanse ;
     Ten hens—all were ' clucks,'
     That is, ' laying hens.'

" Twenty catties of thread, ten ditto of yarn,
To sew up a rent, or a hole neatly darn.
A washerman's stone of the purest white jade ;
A couple of beaters, of date-tree wood made.
She also brought with her ten lumps of sycee,
And nine strings of cash, of the reign of Kang-hsi*

---

* These cash are very much prized on account of the
purity of the metal.

" In two immense bundles her clothing was placed,
With two foreign sashes to tie round the waist;
Two long fur robes—these would fetch a good price;
Three large iron pans—each would cook seven men's
    rice;
A scouring-brush, stiffer and better than cloth;
A cullender, also, to strain off the broth.

" Two tables, four stools, four chairs, and a chest;
Four pieces of calico—these were undressed;
A click-clacking loom, broidered screens for the door,
And of shot-satin coverlets nearly a score;
A fine troupe of players—in fact, the *élite*
Of the stage—with their wardrobe, &c. complete.

" 'Twas my special duty to look after these,
While *she* stayed at home just as grand as you please;
I took care of the money this troupe earned at fairs,
My wife she did nothing but give herself airs.

" My first wife, on her death-bed, committed to my care
A boy and girl—our children—and also made me swear
That I would guard them from all harm; I took a
    solemn oath
To do so—but my second wife, alas! detested both.

13

"Returning home one day, I found the children had
    been beat,
She was raging like a fiend, *they* cowering at her feet;
I remonstrated with her—the children ran and hid;
She screamed, 'I'll see who's mistress here!' And what
    d'ye think she did?

"With a bludgeon she took the watch-dog's life,
The donkey she stabbed with a kitchen-knife;
She dashed out the brains of the flat-billed ducks,
And wrung the necks of the ten poor clucks.

"She burnt the ten catties of cotton yarn,
And the thread she had brought to sew and darn;
The washerman's stone of pure white jade
She smashed, and a number of small ones made.

"By means of a chopper with skill applied,
The beaters were split up and multiplied;
And as for the ten lumps of white sycee,
And the strings of cash of the reign of Kanghsi,
She flung 'em, one after another, at me!

"The bundles in which all her clothing was placed,
She burnt, with the sashes to tie round the waist.
Her two fur robes she tore up in a trice;
Smashed the three pans that each would cook
    seven men's rice.

" The brush and the cullender next my wife seized,
And burnt. Still her anger was far from appeased,—
She chopped up the tables, the stools, and the
chairs,
And the chest, too, soon needed some trifling
repairs.

" She tore into rags the undressed calico,
And shivered the click-clacking loom with one
blow;
The coverlets burnt in a heap on the floor,
And tore into tatters the screens for the door.
Neck and crop out of doors the players she turned,
And the whole of their wardrobe, &c. burned.

" Having vented her rage in this horrible style,
She smiled on her work a demoniac smile;
And while I stood there contemplating the wreck,
She ran off, and hung herself up by the neck.

" I wrote to her friends of her *felo-de-se*.
They came, and of course, laid the blame upon me;
Then rushed off at once to the magistrate's court,
And made of the case a most awful report.

" I bribed right and left—the magistrate first; —
He was bad, I admit, but he wasn't the worst;
His lictors and runners, and writers—what not—
Soon managed to fleece me of all that I'd got.

13 *

"Fields, gardens, and orchards — in short, my
    estate—
All went—my two carriages shared the same fate ;
My three mules, my donkey, pigs, fowls, ducks and
    geese,
I sold, in the hope their proceeds would buy peace.

" 'Twas settled at last, but I found, to my cost,
In gaining the case, I'd my property lost;
Worse still, my poor children both sickened and
    died.—
I think, sir, you'll own that I've been sorely tried.

" The cause of my grief and distress you now know;
Sir, have I not reason to give way to woe ? "
I told him he had—" what else could I say ? "
So I gave him a trifle and went on my way."

————

MORAL.

A word of advice—it's short, but it's true—
I hope no one here will forget it :—
" Don't marry a widow ; as sure as you do,
Take my word, you will always regret it."

THE WATER TEST.*

Quicker—more quick,
Faster still twirls the stick
'Gainst the sides of the *kang*† with an ominous click.
Don't pause, 'tis much best
Not to let the stick rest,
For the faster 'tis twirled the truer the test.
Round and round two strange objects whirl—
The head of a youth and the head of a girl !

---

* This circumstance occurred some few years ago at a village named 青龍橋 (Ch'ing lung chiao), distant from Peking about twenty *li* in a westerly direction from the Hsi chih gate, 西直門. The husband is still living.

† A large earthenware water vessel.

Now they whirl round the side,
Now they separate wide,
Now both of them into the centre are drawn ;
Now they meet face to face
And seem to embrace ;
A moment's pause, and again they whirl on.
On they go in their horrible whirl—
The head of the youth and the head of the girl !

How came that pair
Of ghastly heads there ?
What was the reason their blood had been shed ?
A wronged husband's knife
Had taken the life
Of an unfaithful wife,
Her paramour too, and had cut off each head.
On they go in their horrible whirl—
The head of the youth and the head of the girl !

How the water hisses and seethes,
Tinged as it is with the purple gore
Of the faithless wife and her paramour,
As round the sides of the *kang* it wreathes ;
Forming a whirlpool round which spin
The ghastly heads till they're both sucked in.

In their eyes what an awful glare,
As their faces meet in that mimic abyss,
And seem to unite in a horrible kiss—
How at each other they scowl and stare !

What a mingled look of hate and woe,
Of fright and guilt, those glazed eyes show !

Now they madly whirl round the side ;
   On they speed in their fantastic race,
   Sometimes showing an upturned face
Livid and bruised and scarified !
What an awful expression the features wore
Of the faithless wife and her paramour !

         The girl is fair,
         With long black hair,
And scarcely out of her teens appears ;
      The lad one can see
      Is not older than she,
He cannot have numbered yet twenty years.
Round the sides of the *kang* they whirl—
The head of the lad and the head of the girl !

         The test soon will show
         If they're guilty or no—
And the fact of their guilt is discovered in this :—
         They turn face to face
         And prove their disgrace,
If the lips of the two heads unite in a kiss.
Round the sides of the *kang* they whirl—
The head of the lad and the head of the girl !

Stay your hand for a time,
Let us see if the crime
They are charged with—adultery—really is true ;
Close the lid of the *kang*,
The water ere long
Will be still—we then shall see what the heads do.
Round the sides of the *kang* they whirl—
The head of the lad and the head of the girl!

The water gradually slackens until
In the course of time it is perfectly still.
Raise up the lid, let us now look within :—
'Tis as plain as if both had been caught in their sin!
The wife and her lover are face to face—
In death they acknowledge their guilt and disgrace.
Throw them forth—they are carrion filthy and vile!
Let their curst heads no longer the water defile!
They're convicted of guilt, the test has been tried,
And the husband who slew them is now justified.

MURDER WILL OUT.

Not a long time ago there occurred in Peking
What most will pronounce a remarkable thing!
I'll relate it : for really it proves beyond doubt
The truth of the saying, that "murder will out."

After waiting all day without getting a fare,
A carter was going off home in despair,
When an old fellow hailed him, and bidding him wait,
Climbed into his cart near the Victory Gate.

" Please, Sir," asked the carter, " which way shall I
    drive ? "
"To the south," cried the old man; "now, then, look
    alive ! "
He. *did* look alive, and 'twas pleasant to see
How cheerful the poor carter now seemed to be.

The old mule indulged in a long swinging trot,
But she suddenly stopped in a dark, lonely spot.
This the carter imputed to mischief or spite,
But the mule knew much better — 'twas out of sheer
    fright.

" This is strange," said the man; " what the deuce is
    amiss ?
The old mule has never before been like this."|
Coaxing, swearing, and flogging, he each in turn tried ;
But the mule stood, as if all her legs had been tied.

" You had better get out," cried the carter, much chafed.
His fare remaiued still, and no answer vouchsafed.
"Get out! Are ye deaf ?"—here he turned round his
    head,
And perceived that the old man had fallen back—dead.

This, then, was the reason the mule wouldn't go:
Her instinct had told her a corpse was *de trop*.
For the very same reason for which the mule stopped,
The carter would gladly have run till he dropped.

In a cold perspiration and trembling with fear,
The carter remembered a watch-house was near.
He shouted aloud, till he made himself hoarse,
But the watch were asleep—as a matter of course.

The carter, himself, to the watch-house now ran,
And brought back two watchmen to guard the dead man,
While he hastened off and reported the case,
And conducted the magistrate back to the place.

The corpse was now placed by the side of the road ;
And the mule, thus relieved from her horrible load,
Got over her fright and dashed off in a trot,
Growing bolder the farther she got from the spot.

The magistrate said, when he heard the man's tale,
He would go at the first break of dawn, without fail ;
He was too busy now—besides, 'twas too late ;
And as for the watchmen and corpse—they must wait.

The two men, meanwhile, sat there watching the dead,
    And the time dragged its way slowly on ;
It grew darker and darker ; the clouds overhead
Portended a storm ;—they were both filled with dread—
    What a long time the carter seemed gone !

The cold air of night struck a chill to their bones ;
    They trembled with cold and with fear ;
The wind wailed a dirge, too, in sad plaintive tones,
And, in fancy, they heard quite a chorus of groans
    From a graveyard, alas ! much too near.

'Twas midnight ; the body lay quiet and still ;—
    On the whole, that was " so far so good ; "
His presence, alone made the two men feel chill,—
They shivered—they *would* have a fire, come what *will* ;
    So they went off to gather some wood.

They returned, made a fire with the wood they had found,
    And sat in its warm, ruddy glare ;
When one of the watchmen by chance looking round,
Gave a cry of dismay, and sprang up from the ground—
    The corpse of the man wasn't there !

Yes, while they were busy in gathering sticks,
The corpse had been up to some outlandish tricks.
It had gone ; and the watchmen were now in a fix !
    When the magistrate heard of the case,
Though they told him the truth, he'd declare 'twas a lie.
" I've got it ! " quoth one ; " suppose you and I
Steal a fresh-coffined corpse from the graveyard close by,
    And substitute *that* in his place ! "

Off they started at once, " for they'd no time to waste,—
Broke open a new-looking coffin in haste,
And took out the corpse, which they carefully placed
    On the ground where the other had been.
This done, they sat down without saying a word,
Surprised and astonished at what had occurred ;
There they sat by the fire then, and never once stirred,
    Till the magistrate came on the scene.

But, oh ! who can picture the scene which took place,
When the magistrate bade them uncover the face—
At seeing a maiden scarce eighteen years old !
The sight made the blood of the stoutest run cold.

For round her white neck was a dark streak of blue—
A sign she'd been strangled ; her arms were bruised too,
As if she had struggled but been overpowered
By one who was murderer, ruffian, and coward.

This horrible sight, it is needless to say,
Filled the two watchmen with dread and dismay,
And, thinking for once the bare truth would be best,
Each, without hesitation, soon made a clean breast.

His Worship, believing their tale to be true,
Conceived he had now got one end of a clue ;
This he traced with such consummate skill, that at last
He knew, and had got, the girl's murderer fast.

It seems, the girl's father—his wife being dead—
Had recently taken it into his head
To purchase another, his old age to cheer—
Little dreaming his purchase would cost him so dear.

The person by whom his new wife had been sold
Was her husband—although the old man had been told
They were brother and sister, and, as such was the case,
No harm could ensue should he visit the place.

He came at all hours, when the merchant was out ;
Yet the old man was free from suspicion or doubt.
But not so the girl, she detected their plan,
And watched them, unheeding the risk that she ran.

Her father soon after left home for a week,
And the two now determined their vengeance to wreak
On her who had seen through their villainous schemes :—
They strangled the girl, spite of struggles and screams.

All signs of the murderous deed were effaced,
And the corpse of the girl in a coffin was placed ;
This was put in the graveyard, and now the vile pair
Feeling safe from suspicion, went home free from care.

On the father's return he was told by his wife
That his daughter had died of a fever then rife.
This the wife told with tears, and the father, though
    grieved,
The base woman's plausible story believed.

The murderers met with the fate they deserved ;
They had strangled the girl—they themselves were thus
    served.
Thus strangely was brought a vile murder to light,
Through the trance of a man and a stubborn mule's
    fright.

This story is done ; it remains but to tell,
That the old fellow soon turned up, hearty and well ;
He was subject to fits, and while in one of those,
The old mule had jibbed—hence the blunder arose.

While the watchmen were absent collecting the wood,
The old man had roused, and at once understood
That the carter had left him there, thinking him dead.
He knew better, and getting up, trudged home to bed.

The finger of Heaven we distinctly can trace
From beginning to end of this singular case ;
Each actor and act, one can see, too, quite plain,
Were but separate links in His wonderful chain.

THE EARTHEN TEA-POT.

When the Sung sovereigns, eight hundred years ago,
Ruled over China,—at the famed Ting chou
There lived a worthy merchant, named *Li-'hao*,
Together with a magistrate, named *Pao*.

Both men were popular and much admired;
One for his wealth—by industry acquired—
The other for his wisdom, skill, and tact,
And even justice of his every act.

One day the merchant a short journey made
Into the country, on affairs of trade.
Returning homewards with a purse well-lined,
And being in a happy frame of mind,
He blandly thought that he could do no less
Than take a glass to wet his late success.

He did so. Had he but been content
With that one glass, and on his journey went,
Then all were well, he had got home all right,
And slept securely in his bed that night;
But that one glass sharpened his appetite.

He drank it up; but soon he craved for more,
Nor left, till he'd imbibed some half-a-score;
He then proceeded on his homeward way—
Going but slowly too, for sooth to say,
At every inn he felt compelled to stop
And quench his thirst—with " just another drop;"
Until at last, when nearly at Ting chou,
The drink on *Li 'hao's* frame began to show;
He staggered on a bit, when down he fell;—
What happened him the next few lines will tell.

A potter, named *Chou,*
Had occasion to go
To his kiln, to attend to and make up his fires;
As he passed, the mere sight
Of *Li 'hao's* drunken plight
Stirred up in his breast avaricious desires.

For he saw, peeping out from the drunken man's waist,
A purse. Still *Li 'hao* never stirred.
" There's no one in sight." *Chou* snatched it in haste,
And the purse to his own waist transferred.

14

But then came the thought, " The moment he wakes "
   (Here he trembled in every limb)
" He'll miss it.   Suppose strict inquiry he makes,
   And the crime should be traced home to him ? "

The thought of discovery filled him with dread—
   The theft was with great danger fraught.
" Shall I kill him ?   No tales can be told by the dead."
   (Even now, he had killed him in thought.)

The theft had been done, murder came in its train ;
   He determined the poor wretch should die.
" But how ? "   In a moment it flashed through his
     brain,—
   " I'll burn him, my kiln is close by."

The senseless *Li'hao* to the kiln he conveyed,
And the ill-fated man in the furnace next laid ;
Then igniting the fuel, the door he closed-to,
And shut out the still living man from his view.

" God! what a fearful cry !   My very heart
Stayed its pulsations for a time, and then
Appeared as if 'twere knocking 'gainst my breast
To quit so vile a place.

" Faugh !   What a smell of roasting flesh !
The summer air seems laden with its
Sickening scent.   The passing breeze,
To my distempered fancy, breathes
Only murder.
The very birds, on every tree and bough,
Seem but to twitter '*murder*,' and ' *Li 'hao.*' "

The fire blazed up fiercely, it crackled and seethed ;
Through the flues of the kiln a faint atmosphere
   wreathed,
Which slowly rose up in the evening sky,
And appeared like a film to the murderer's eye.

Soon nothing remained save a few calcined bones ;
These he pounded to ashes between two large stones ;
Then the ashes he mixed with some clay, which he got,
And made of the mixture an earthen tea-pot.

When the earthen pot into the furnace was placed,
He felt certain the murder could never be traced ;
" Who would dream that the corpse of the ill-fated man
Would ever be used as a pot or a pan ? "

The pot was soon baked ; he'd the money secure ;
No one could suspect him, of that he felt sure :
So he hurried off homewards, nor once did he stop,
Till he'd placed the tea-pot on a shelf in his shop.

14 *

"Straw shoes! Straw shoes!"
For poor folks to use,
Who cotton or silk cannot buy.
Those who like their shoes neat,
And set well to the feet,
Come here, and old *Chang's* straw shoes try!

"Here you are, neat and strong!
There's no telling how long
They'll last, if they're treated with care.
You had better make haste,
And not precious time waste—
Buy my straw shoes, at one tiao a pair!"

While hawking his shoes, *Chang* drew near the door
Of his old friend the potter's small crockery store;
'Twas so long ago since he'd passed by the shop,
That he stared with surprise, then he came to a stop.
No wonder, indeed, that he stood still to view it—
The place was so changed that old *Chang* hardly knew it.

"Ho! ho!" murmured he, "*Chou* looks pretty thriving,
No doubt he's a capital business driving.
Let me see, the last pair of shoes that he had
He has not paid for yet—this is really too bad!
As I'm passing the shop, here, I may as well get it;
If he hasn't the money—why, then, I'll outset it."

Chang entered the shop and demanded his debt ;
The potter replied, " I can't pay you just yet."
Then said *Chang*, " I'll outset it. Let's see what you've
     got.
I'll cry quits if you give me that earthen tea-pot."
" Agreed ! " cried the potter ; " by all means pray take
     it."
(He'd often and often been tempted to break it,
But something restrained him—it wasn't the price—
But it *would be so like killing one person twice.*)

This pot to *Chang's* comfort would largely conduce—
And that fact alone made him choose it ;
So he took it off home, filled it ready for use,
And that night had occasion to use it.

Out of bed he soon got,
And laid hold of the pot—
Little knew he the storm that was brewing—
When a voice from within,
Roared out, " Don't begin !
" That's my nose ! What the deuce are you doing? "

Chang sat down in a fright ;
Looked round left and right—
Im fact, every place but the right one ;
Quoth the pot, " I am here.
Take me up ; do not fear ;
There's nothing in me to affright one."

Seeing *Chang* hesitate,
The pot grew irate,
And bawled, " Do at once as I bid you!
Don't stand like a dunce ;
Take me up, Sir, at once ! —
So you thought to make use of me, did you ?

" Now, I'll make use of *you*,
And to some purpose too.
Stand me down on the bed.   Now, sit near me."
Chang tremblingly did
Whate'er he was bid.
" That'll do," cried the pot. " Now, then, hear me."

" You think I'm a pot ;
I assure you I'm not—
Or rather, I ought not to *be* one.
Did you e'er see a man
Like a pot or a pan ?
Look intently at *me*, and you'll *see* one.

" This may seem strange to you,
But though strange, it is true,
I was made what you see by a potter ;
You have often heard tell
Of the place they call hell—
That is hot—but his furnace was hotter."

Here the earthen pot told the whole facts of the case—
How he took the first glass, and to what it soon led,
His horrible death—everything that took place
From the time of his journey till put on that bed.

Chang gazed at the pot, and distinctly could trace
On its surface the lines of the murdered man's face;
But the most astonishing thing of the lot,
He could not only see the nose, mouth, and eyes
Of the ill-fated man, but could now recognize,
Jumbled up in a strange indescribable way—
Condensed, as it were—how, *Chang* couldn't say—
The whole of *Li 'hao* in the earthen tea-pot.

On hearing the tale,
Chang grew ghastly pale;
But he grew paler still when the tea-pot requested
He would go straight to court,
And the murder report.
(Against this proceeding *Chang* stoutly protested.
They might think it a hoax,
And they don't admire jokes—
And a magistrate's court was a place he detested.)

It took a long time for the pot to persuade him;
It threatened at first, then it promised to aid him.
On this understanding, *Chang* gave his consent,
And next day, with the pot, to the magistrate went.

First placing the pot at the door of the court,
Chang entered, and kneeling, soon made his report :
That on such and such day, in such and such place—
(Here he fully related the whole of the case).

When he'd finished the story, His Worship averred,
'Twas the queerest adventure he ever had heard ;
And bade the clerk write it all down, word for word.
" Go," said he to old *Chang*, " bring the witness this
    way,
And I'll hear what the earthen tea-pot has to say."
Chang went off and fetched the tea-pot from the door,
And his witness he carefully placed on the floor.

Quoth the magistrate, " Answer me truly, Tea-pot ;
Is it true what old *Chang* has just told me, or not?
Are you really and truly the murdered *Li 'hao?*
Speak up ! If you are, you shall have justice now."

Not a word spoke the pot ; this seemed very queer.
His Worship was wroth ; *Chang* trembled with fear,
And cried, as he stirred the pot up with his foot,
" For goodness' sake, answer the question that's put !"

" What's up with the pot ? Why the deuce don't it
    speak ?
Does it think I'll keep on at this scene for a week ?
Once for all, will you speak ? " No reply could be got
By His Worship or *Chang* from the earthen tea-pot.

The pot was alternately threatened and coaxed,—
The bystanders thought that His Worship was hoaxed;
And so did *he* too : one could easily see,
By the scowl on his face, what the upshot would be.

He roared out to *Chang*, " You may think this is sport!
You'll alter your mind, though, before you leave court.
Drag him out, with his pot! But before the wretch
 goes,
Throw him down, and administer forty sound blows."

" Harder still! " cried His Worship. " I'll soon let
 him see,
If he'll venture to play his vile tricks upon me! "
The lictors thus urged, did not spare poor old *Chang*,
But laid on their blows what is termed " hot and
 strong."

By the time they were finished he felt pretty sore,
Worse still when they "*footed*" him out at the door;
He taxed the tea-pot with perfidiousness,
For wilfully leading him into this mess.

Quoth the pot, " You have only yourself got to blame.
Do you think, though a pot, I'm devoid of all shame?
Had I clothes on—though only a jacket or cloak—
When it came to the push I'd·have certainly spoke.

" Wrap me up in your coat and again take me in.
Come, do as I bid you—don't stand there and grin !
This time you will find you've no cause for alarm ;
Now enter, at once, with me under your arm."

Chang obeyed, though he didn't half relish the job—
He'd a notion His Worship might take off his nob,
Which proceeding did *not* coincide with his views ;
But ordered to enter, he dared not refuse.

Chang entered the court, and the same as before,
The earthen tea-pot he placed down on the floor.
When he saw this, His Worship exclaimed, " I'll be
      shot,
If here isn't the fellow come back with the pot !

" Not content with the flogging he 's already had,
He 's come back for some more ;—this is really too bad !
Once he 's fooled me, but let him again try that trick,
And I swear he'll get something far worse than the
      stick ! "

" Your Worship," cried *Chang*, " the last time we came,
The tea-pot was silent, from motives of shame.
That's past : if Your Worship will question it now,
You'll soon be convinced *it's* the murdered *Li 'hao.*"

Pao questioned the pot, which now told its tale,
The recital of which made the hearers grow pale.
When the story was ended the magistrate swore
He would bring the crime home to the murderer's door.

The potter was seized, but the crime he denied.
Pao beckoned his men, and they torture applied;
But finding no torture would make him confess,
His Worship resolved to resort to *finesse*.

Chou was placed in a cell, his wife was then brought;
Pao soon on the woman's simplicity wrought:—
She must speak the whole truth, and above all take heed,
For her husband already had owned to the deed.

The woman, conceiving this tale to be true,
Without hesitation told all that she knew,
And that she had the purse—" That'll do ! " exclaimed
  Pao,
" Your husband will probably own to it now."

On hearing these words, the poor woman perceived
That she'd been by the magistrate grossly deceived ;
She had fall'n in the trap which His Worship had laid,
And, unconscious of harm, had her husband betrayed.

The potter was brought to the yamên once more,
And his guilt he as firmly denied as before.
" So you will," cried His Worship, " your guilt still
    deny ?
Your wife has confessed, so you've no need to lie."

The potter, on finding his wife had confessed,
In turn, to the magistrate, made a clean breast :
He had robbed and burnt *Li 'hao* while drunk and
    asleep—
He owned it—and as he had sown he must reap.

His Worship, the moment the potter had ceased,
Condemned him to death,—his wife he released ;
Then he gave twenty taels to old *Chang*, on the spot,
And solemnly buried the earthen tea-pot.

THE BORROWED BRIDE.

In the reign of *Tao-kuang*,
Near the town of Niuchuang,
Lived a farmer by name *Li-tzu-chiu;*
He'd no care on his hands,
For he'd houses and lands,
And was what might be termed " well-to-do."
He besides had a wife,
A cosy old dame,
And a daughter—the little *Tai-hsiao.*
But the daughter, alas!
Brought the old folks to shame.
If you'll listen I'll try to tell how.
Ai ya! Ai yo!
What can parents expect
Who their children neglect?
Ten chances to one they don't turn out correct.
Tai-hsiao was betrothed
To *Hu-lin,* whom she loathed;
But she greatly young *Tê-hsi* admired,

A good-looking lad,
Yet—'twas really too bad—
A mere house-boy her father had hired.
The two met every day
In a clandestine way;
This continued for nearly a year,
'Till at length, to be brief,
To the girl's shame and grief,
Strange symptoms began to appear.
Ai ya! Ai yo!
Here was a state for *Tai-hsiao* to be in!
Enciente with *Tê-hsi*, yet betrothed to *Hu-lin*.

Little *Tai-hsiao*, in this dreadful strait,
Ai-ya'd and ai-yo'd at a pitiful rate,
In vain bewailing her wretched fate,
Repenting too, but a trifle too late.
She could eat no food,
But would sit and brood,
Or steal away to some solitude.

*　　　*　　　*　　　*　　　*

Her mother, who had her full share of sagacity,
And was, moreover, blessed with a keen perspicacity,
One day saw, what was plain to the meanest capacity,
The state of poor little *Tai-hsiao*.
Much enraged at her daughter's low state of morality,
Which soon must be known, too, throughout the locality,
She screamed, " Tell me, girl, without further formality,
How you came in the plight you are now! "

Her invectives she uttered with great volubility,
For she was expert in all kinds of scurrility;
Dilated at length on the girl's culpability,
 Betraying her rage on her face.
The dame wagged her tongue with alarming rapidity.
She devoured all the frightful details with avidity,
Her features assuming a stolid rigidity,
 As she entered at once on the case.

" Tell me, *Tai-hsiao*—I insist upon knowing;
 I'm determined to fathom this mystery out—
To what is your pale face and moping ways owing?
 Tell the truth, girl, at once—don't stand there and
 pout."

Tai-hsiao drooped her head—she felt the blood dyeing
 Her neck, cheeks, and brow, a most brilliant red.
In this strange dilemma she burst out a-crying,
 And 'midst blushes and sobbing she tremblingly said:

" I don't think I take enough exercise, mother—
 Rich food perhaps makes me dyspeptic as well;
My dulness arises from one cause or 'tother,
 It may be from both, but indeed I can't tell."

" 'Tisn't thus," cried the dame. " Do you think I can't
 see?
So don't try to palm off that tale upon me;
You hardened young jade, you may well pipe your eye—
Where do you hope to go when you come to die?

"You shameless young hussy! Oh, what shall I do?
You've ruined yourself and your family too.
Drat the girl!" and here the old dame, in a huff,
Cried, "Take that—that—and that!"—the *that* being a
    cuff.

"Tell me (cuff) who is the (cuff) author of all this dis-
    grace?
Let me know (cuff), and I'll leave my nail-marks on his
    face."
In this fix poor *Tai-hsiao* at once made a clean breast,
And her intrigue with *Té-hsi* to her mother confessed.

The dame's face grew crimson with anger and shame,
And she lustily screamed out on hearing the name:
"What! *Té-hsi!* My daughter intrigue with that beast!
A house-boy! She might have looked higher, at least."

In the height of the squabble the father returned,
    Exclaiming, "Hallo! what's the cause of this row
'Twixt mother and child?" From the old dame he learned
    The intrigue of *Té-hsi* with little *Tai-hsiao*.

On hearing the tale, he stamped, raged, and swore.
    "He would skin the young whelp;" but concluding
    it best
To first catch *Té-hsi*,—so he made for the door,
    And searched high and low; but the lad was *non est*.

His designs on *Tê-hsi* being baulked,
    He again took to storming and raving ;
Back again to the parlour he stalked,
    Looking anything else but engaging.
Then, much to poor *Tai-hsiao's* dismay,
    He indulged for a time in invective,—
Inquired what the neighbours would say
    When they heard she was found so defective
Of that virtue without which mere beauty is dross,
Entailing increasing regret at its loss.

Said he, " You base girl ! you deserve to be licked."
    And without any more hesitation
He clutched at her hair, and was going to inflict
    A sound, but deserved castigation—

When a noise from without " smote his ear,"
    Staying the falling blow ;
He listened, and quaking with fear,
    At once let her go.
He went to the door to ascertain why
    Or what was the cause
Of the noise, when a sight " struck his eye "
    Which caused him to pause.

There, entering the door, was *Hu's* negociator ;
L- u-chiu stood looking on—a thunderstruck spectator.

15

Four friends were with the go-between, behind them men were bearing
Betrothal presents ;—on the scene a motley crowd were staring.

Eight cases containing
Clothing of every sort—
Head-gear, jewellery—in short,
All things appertaining
To the outfit of a bride.
In the banquetting line,
Were two jars of wine,
And two roasted pigs, side by side ;
Six score of large cakes ; besides these, in fact,
A large hamper with all sorts of dainties was packed.

Li-tzu-chiu felt vexed and irate,
But mustered up courage and went to the gate ;
Bowing and scraping, each guest he invited
To partake of his cheer, as if highly delighted.
To each guest a cup
Of tea was served up,
'Twixt talking and smoking to leisurely sup.
Hu's father then bowed,
And solemnly vowed
That he felt at this moment remarkably proud.
" My son *Hu*," said he,
" Will most happy be
In his union with *Tai-hsiao*, the daughter of *Li*."

Oh! little he knew
The intended of *Hu*
Had already lost face, to his son proved untrue.
This was yet to be learnt.
Meanwhile, to proceed,
The paper was burnt,
The bearers well fee'd,
And *Li* was soon freed
From the presence of *Hu*.
He inwardly grieved
He'd the presents received;
But what could he do?

Of course we all know that he should have rejected
The presents, and spoken the truth like a man.
He did the reverse—he the presents accepted;
We should all do the same, contradict me who can.

'Tis easy to say that we should or we shouldn't,
This proceeding run down, or that thing abuse;
We shouldn't have acted thus—oh, no! we couldn't,—
But I'd like to see some of us placed in his shoes.

The time passed rapidly away,
And nearer drew the wedding day.
Old *Li-tzu-chiu*,
In a regular stew,
His worry increasing the nearer it drew.
Poor *Tai-hsiao* kept
To her own room, and wept,
And but seldom over its threshold stept.

15 *

Nearer and nearer the wedding day drew ;
Paler and paler the poor damsel grew.
What can be done in so dreadful a case ?
How can we hide such a shocking disgrace ?
Suppose when she's wed—on the actual day—
Tai-hsiao is confined—what can we say ?
The bare mention alone made *Li* droop his head ;
But the dame thought a bit, then she suddenly said :—

     " I have it, my dear !
     I can see my way clear !
     I 've just hit on a scheme,
     Which, though strange it may seem,
     Will carry us through,
     If well managed by you.
     Now, don't say a word
     Till my plan you have heard.

" Our bailiff, *Sun-ssu*, has a daughter, *Luan-ying*,
She 's exactly seventeen and will be just the thing ;
We must borrow this damsel to take *Tai-hsiao's* place
At the wedding, and thus we shall hide our disgrace."

" Psha ! " blurted out *Li*, " why, whoever heard
Of borrowing a girl ?   The thing 's too absurd ! "
" Not quite so absurd as you fancy," said she ;
" It can safely be managed—but leave that to me.

" To look at the two, one might solemnly swear
They were twins—that one dame had given birth to the
     pair ;
They are both of one age, and as like as two peas,
And one can pass off for the other, with ease.

" We must borrow this girl, 'tis our only resource ;
Dress her up as the bride—'twill be awkward, of course ;
She must take our girl's place there, at least for a time.
She 's poor, so of course it 's no very great crime.

" On the ninth the sham bride can come back to our place*
As if 'twere her home—thus we hide our disgrace ;
Tai-hsiao, who ere then will have been brought to bed,
And no doubt recovered, can go back instead."

Li, who had listened hitherto to his wife with rapt attention,
Here broke in with "Allow me, dear, just casually to
  mention,

---

* At daybreak on the ninth day after marriage, one
or more of the relatives—generally the parents—of the
bride go to the house of the bridegroom and escort the
girl back to her maiden home; this is called '*hui-mên*, returning to the door. It is optional with the bridegroom
whether he accompanies them or not, but he must visit
them during the day; he then kotows to the bride's
parents, and makes their personal acquaintance for the
first time. In the evening the bride returns to her husband's house; after this they can visit one another's
homes without ceremony, and as it suits their convenience.
  It is not to be supposed for a moment that they could
possibly exchange the girls without the knowledge of the
husband; they know, or fancy, he will be compelled to hold
his peace for fear of the disgrace he will bring on his own
family if he does not conceal it.

The conscience of *Sun-ssu* perhaps is particularly tender,—
We may want to borrow, but the thing is, will he lend
   her ? "

" You are raising up obstacles where there are none ;
   Good hard cash," said the wife, " will soon buy him.
By hook or by crook, it has got to be done,
   So you had better at once go and try him."

       " But, my dear Mrs. *Li*,"
         Pleaded he,
          " Don't you see ?
      Sun-ssu may refuse
     To lend her to me,
     And not choose
That his girl in this way should be wedded.
     " 'Tis only for nine days, or so,
       But you know
     Such a question as this
     He might well take amiss,
For he is rather, what I call hot-headed.
Should he fly in a rage and kick up a row,
There 's an end of the wedding of *Hu* with *Tai-hsiao*."

" That 's easily managed," replied the old dame,
" He 's fond of a cup, like some more I can name ;
You just ask him in, and well ply him with wine,—
You can manage that, surely, it 's quite in your line.

" Chat pleasantly with him of this thing or that,—
    The state of the weather, the country, the crops ;
Throw out a few hints, for he 's poor as a rat,—
    You can do what you like when he 's once in his drops.

" When you see he 's well primed, broach the subject at
    once—
For the loan of his daughter you'll give fifty taels.
If he doesn't agree, you may call me a dunce ;
    I 'll stake my existence that money prevails."

'Twas quite plain that *Li* had no will of his own,
    But like a good husband he used her's instead.
He had better have left such a wild scheme alone ;
    As it was, like a bear by the nose he was led.

    He was easily persuaded ;
    With heart and soul the plan he aided ;
    Sun-ssu immediately invited,
    Who entered, feeling much delighted
    At his cordial reception ;
      And, as he frankly told his wife,
    " This was, indeed, without exception,
    The proudest moment of his life."

Li commenced, " My friend, be seated."
Sun had never been so treated ;
He bowed, and in a chair dropped shyly.
Li, the meantime watching slyly,

Mulled some wine, and helped *Sun* freely,
  Who received it, nothing loth.
At first he sipped it quite genteelly ;
  Grown bold, he drank enough for both.

Li spoke of this, and that, and t'other,
Called him " friend " and " worthy brother,"
Just the sort of friend he needed—
None felt the want so much as he did.
Then, with tact and skill unerring,
  He spoke of secrets—wished advice—
Laid quite a sprat to catch a herring—
  The bait was gobbled in a trice.

Sun, whose voice was getting thicker
Through deep devotion to the liquor,
Here with moistened eye besought him,
If indeed a friend he thought him,
To tell him plainly all about it,
  On his fidelity depend.
Cried he, " Though poor, you needn't doubt it,
  I 'll prove myself a trusty friend."

With quivering voice and tones dramatic,
Li told the tale in language graphic,
From the very first beginning—
How the dreadful fruit of sinning
Each day ripened—'twas appalling!
  At any time they might expect
Tai-hsiao to have a brat whose squalling
  Would trumpet forth the damning fact !

On hearing this catastrophe, *Sun* fairly roared with
   laughter;
" Ho! ho! Ha! ha! I say," said he, " what the dickens
   are you after ?
I really can't perceive your drift, I can't upon the life of
   me !
Unless your notion is to make a dowdy old midwife of me!

" *Tai-hsiao that* way! upon my word, that is indeed sur-
   prising ;"
And here he gave a grunt, and tried to look quite sym-
   pathising.
" Were it any other thing than that, a word of yours would
   turn me,
But such a case as this, I think, can't possibly concern me."

" *That* don't concern you," answered *Li*, " but hold your
   tongue a minute ;
I 've something else that does, though, or else the deuce is
   in it.
To-morrow is her wedding-day — by then she'll be a
   mother—
You see I 'm in a hobble, either one way or the other.

" There is but one way out of it, that is, if I could borrow
Your daughter for a week or two, commencing from to-
   morrow ;

She could personate my daughter then—it wouldn't be
    suspected—
And on the ninth, when she came home, the change could
    be effected."*

> *Sun* sprang to his feet,
> Kicking over his seat,
> With a face that betrayed opposition;
> Said he, " You old cur!
> What am I to infer
> From such a—a—a base proposition?

> " Borrow my daughter, will ye!
> You old wretch, I 'll kill ye! "
> Here he began roaring out,
> Chairs and tables kicked about;
> Stamping, swearing, breaking, crashing,
> Liquor spilling, crockery smashing!

> " Let mine go!—that 's cool!
> Do I look like a fool?
> Do you think for a moment I 'd let her?
> If your own 's come to shame,
> You've yourself got to blame,
> You ought to have brought her up better! "

---

* *See* note p. 229.

At this unearthly hubbub *Li* was perfectly aghast;
He clapped his hand on *Sun-ssu's* mouth, and got him still
    at last.
"For goodness' sake, do have some sense, don't let the
    neighbours know;
I don't want the girl for nothing, you shall have a *quid
    pro quo!*"

Seeing *Sun* about to speak, he cried out "Not a word!
Don't hazard an opinion until the whole you've heard.
I'll give you fifty taels at once; besides, five *mu* of land
I'll let you have for ten years, and not a *cash* demand.

"Think over all the pros and cons—don't be precipitate;
The fifty taels—the bit of land—give each its proper
    weight.
Think over what you're getting now, and finally decide
If you'll lend your daughter for a time to personate the
    bride.

"Still, if you're not agreeable, and my inducement fails,
Some one else, perhaps, may want the land and fifty taels:
Just say the word—do you accept? What, hesitating
    still!
Be quick, or I must toddle off to some one else that will."

Sun bent his head and cogitated,
And mentally ejaculated,
" The ground and money I may just as well accept as not;
I shall be a land proprietor—
As for the girl, I'll quiet her—
Bailiff work, etcetera, then for me may go to pot."

Said he, looking up and grinning,
" What you said at the beginning,
Didn't seem to me, I must confess, to be exactly right;
But after what you've stated,
I must be addle-pated
If I didn't view the matter in a very different light.

" The gifts you needn't mention—
But since 'tis your intention
To give the cash and land to me, of course I can't refuse.
As for the girl, I'll lend her;
Only tell me when to send her.
In the way you've put it now, 'tis quite ' another pair of
    shoes.'

" 'Tis the simplest thing to do it,
There 's but one objection to it,
Should my girl's intended father know, there'd be a
    precious row;
You may take my word upon it,
He would clap his *veto* on it,
And that—if possible—would make the hobble worse than
    now."

" Don't be the least alarmed," said *Li,*
The secret rests with you and me ;
The neighbours needn't know—'tis no business of theirs—
And as for any prying,
Or underhanded spying,
I'd like to catch 'em trying to find out our affairs."

They discussed the matter over from every point of view,
At length they finally arranged on what they ought to do :
Sun should bring the girl at night, explaining all to
her ;
Li should pay the money down—the lease as well transfer.

Luan-ying should dress in bridal clothes, and take his
daughter's place ;
Of course they couldn't find it out, for they wouldn't see
her face.
On the ninth, when she came home, they could be again
exchanged.
Each went his way—the scheme had been agreeably arranged.*

Sun went home quite elated,
To his wife expatiated
On his luck, as lease and money he on the table laid ;
Explained all to the daughter,
Exclaiming that he thought her
A lucky girl, for by this scheme her fortune would be
made.

---

* *See* note p. 229.

What she thought they never heeded—
'Twas the money they both needed ;
She might in vain have pleaded, so she thought she'd
better not.
Then off at once they sent her,
Saw her reach the house and enter,
She determining internally to spoil their little plot.

The wedding morn broke clear and bright,—
Luan-ying from her couch arose ;
The girl had passed a sleepless night,
Brooding in silence o'er her woes.
And now she saw, on looking round,
The wedding portion all laid out ;
Arranged on tables—on the ground—
On all sides—everywhere about.

Boxes, presses,
Filled with dresses,
Some of every sort and kind,
Quilted, wadded, furred, and lined ;
Figured, flowered, plain aud laced,
To suit the fashion or the taste ;
Sashes, garters, stockings, shoes,
And countless things that ladies use,
Pins and needles, head-gear jewels,
A lady's proper working tools.
Toilet-service, looking-glass,
Wash-hand basin made of brass,
Pewter, which like bright silver shone,—
She almost wished they were her own.

The girl was then in *Tai-hsiao's* clothes attired,
  (In truth the bridal vestments well became her).
Soothed by the wily dame, caressed, admired,
She for a time forgot she was but hired,
  And thought she *was* the bride—and who can
    blame her ?
She was so young, so modest, and so pretty,
To lend her thus for money seemed a pity.

Yet there she stood, a living sacrifice,
  Of guilt unconscious—she was but obeying
Her parents' orders, yet at what a price !
Her purity to screen another's vice.
  She was an innocent they were betraying.
In vain might she bewail her sad position,
She had no power to alter her condition.

'Tis six o'clock. See yonder a long procession comes ;
And now they reach the house, amid the crash of gongs
  and drums.*
Tai-hsiao remains within the room, she dare not show her
  face,
And envies in her heart the girl who *pro tem* takes her
  place.

---

  * When the bridal chair arrives it is escorted by musicians beating gongs and drums, blowing trumpets, etc. On the return of the procession, when the bride is in the chair, the music is softer, small gongs, clarionets, flutes, fifes, etc., being used.

Luan-ying, now veiled, is carried, through the hubbub and
    the din,*
To the bridal chair in waiting, and safely placed within ;
To soft and plaintive music the train returns once more,
Bringing the fictitious bride, till they reach the bride-
    groom's door.

The chair is lowered carefully, the girl assisted out
By two officious matrons ; the people round about
Throng nearer, just to get a view ; the bridal carpet's
    spread,†
The girl, supported by the two, within the house is led.

---

   * The bride, closely veiled, is *carried* to the chair,
and placed in it by her father, brother, uncle, or, in case of
her having neither, by her nearest male relative. On her
arriving at the bridegroom's, she *walks* from the chair to
the house.

   † When the chair containing the bride arrives at the
bridegroom's house, a carpet is spread from the chair to
the hall, if the parties are rich ; if they are poor, two short
pieces are used, the bride in her progress alternately stepping on either, the hind one she has just quitted being
hastily raised and again spread in front of her, this being
repeated till she reaches the house. Previous to the bride
quitting the chair, the bridegroom stands outside his door
with a bow and arrow in his hand ; he stretches the bow
to its fullest extent three times, with the arrow pointing
to the chair ; sometimes the bridegroom lets fly at it, this
is done to frighten away her " bad spirits." After this
she is assisted out by two matrons, and supported into the
courtyard, where both bride and bridegroom worship
heaven and earth. The bride is then led towards the door

Heaven and earth were worshipped, every necessary rite
Was gone through most punctiliously. The poor girl
    quaked with fright;
She formed a thousand plans, as the time wore slowly on,
What should she do when night came, and all the guests
    were gone?

---

of the house; on the door-sill is placed an apple, on the top of which is also placed a saddle; this is emblematical of domestic happiness, the two characters, *p'ing-an*, "apple and saddle," having the same sound as p'ing an, "peace, tranquillity," etc. Within the entrance of the door is placed a pan containing live charcoal, implying a hope that the husband may be prosperous. The bride steps first over the saddle, then over the pan of charcoal; she is then led to the *kang*; at the foot of this is a bag containing various cerials, principally millet, step by step may she ascend, or may she be good and prosperous. The bride sits on the *kang*, and the bridegroom standing at its foot takes off her veil with a steelyard or weighing stick; he then ascends the *kang* and sits facing the bride. Each of them are now handed a bowl of small dumplings, containing minced meat of some kind, of which both of them *must* partake—these are nearly raw. The bridegroom's mother then asks them, "Is what you are eating cooked or uncooked?" They will naturally answer "uncooked"; the character used having also the meaning "to bear, to produce," etc., the answer implies a hope that she may bear children. The bridegroom's mother then hands them two goblets tied together with red string, both drink in silence, and the ceremony is complete.

The matrons attending the bride must have husbands and children, and the more children they have, the better it is considered. No widows on any account are allowed to be in attendance.

16

Slowly sank the setting sun,
　Behind the mountains disappearing;
The bright stars shone forth one by one—
　Heaven's myriad eyes were downward peering.

At length none but themselves remained,
　The wedding guests had all departed;
The fact was scarcely ascertained
　When up the bridegroom's mother started,

Exclaiming, as a lamp she lighted,
　" Thank goodness? they've all gone away!
For which, my dear, I am delighted—
　But ain't this been a busy day?

"Lor! how pale the dear child's face is!
　Poor thing! she's tired.　Come along,
My dear; for you the proper place is
　The bed—so I'll spread the kang."

The girl was to an inner chamber led,
　Assisted by her mother in undressing;
Detaching, too, the trinkets from her head,
The dame, when she had made the bridal bed,
　Called in her son, and left them with a blessing.

There stood the bridegroom, there the borrowed
   bride ;
   Both feeling somewhat disconcerted.
He timidly steals to her side,
Embraces her with love and conscious pride ;
   She trembling stands, with face and eyes averted.

What shall she do?   Oh! for some hiding-place !
   Would that the ground would open and receive her !
Where can she run and hide her burning face ?
Is there no method to avert disgrace ?
   How make him, but for a moment, leave her ?

How can she tell him they're not really wed—
   That avarice to this cruel state has brought her ?
A bright idea pops into her head—
She turned, and to the bridegroom trembling said,
   " I am *so* thirsty, please bring me some water."

There was no water in the room, she knew.
   He seized a cup and hastened to obey her,
Off to the kitchen in a moment flew.
She closed the door, the bolt securely drew,
   And sank down, almost fainting, in a chair.

He got the water and was hastening back,
   Groping his way, to keep himself from falling,
Through the dark passage, with extended neck,
When 'gainst the door he ran,—this sudden check
   Not only brought him up, but sent him sprawling.

Up, in a rage, the bridegroom jumped,
   I'm almost afraid the young man swore,
As the closed door he heartily thumped,
   Exclaiming, " Why have you bolted the door ?

" You asked for a drink, the water I brought.
   Had I any idea what you were about,
You'd have fetched it yourself ; but who would have
    thought
   It was done for the purpose of shutting me out ? "

     Cried the girl, " All you tell me,
     Won't coax or compel me
To open the door—I'm not such a fool ;
     Since *you* went to dip it,
     You also may sip it,
You want some cold water your vain love to cool."

     Hu, on this, began bawling,
     His parents both calling,
To whom he explained this most singular case,
     How his wife wanted water,
     Which he'd no sooner brought her
Than she heartlessly bolted the door in his face.

The old couple naturally opened their eyes,
And stared at the lad in blank surprise ;
They called to the girl, " My dear, what 's amiss ?
Why have you treated our boy like this ?
Waking us up with this dreadful row—
We thought much better of you, *Tai-hsiao !* "

The girl broke in with, "It's no such thing!
I'm not *Tai-hsiao!* I'm little *Luan-ying*,
The daughter of *Sun-ssu*, the overseer."
Then cried the couple, "What brings you here?"
The girl, with much sobbing, her story told,
How by her father she had been sold,
How she'd been sent off to take the place
Of little *Tai-hsiao*, who had "lost her face,"
Everything from beginning to end,
Which startled them all, you may well depend.
When the poor girl could tell them no more
She sobbed, "Now you know why I bolted the door."

The old man's face with rage grew red,
"I'll serve the vagabonds out," he said;
"Your father, my dear, is a miserly cur!
And your mother—but there, we won't speak of her.
I don't know which is the worst of the two,
Your father, or that cunning rogue *Li-tzu-chiu.*
And as for that filthy, deceitful *Tai-hsiao*,
She may go to the deuce! *you're* our daughter now.
Whoever you are, you're a good substitute,
And we don't care two straws so long as you suit.
There! now that's all settled, so open the door,
And we'll toddle off to our chamber once more."

Thought the poor little maiden, "Now, what shall I do?
He's not so bad-looking, he's kind-hearted too—
When I wanted the water, how quickly he went;
Perhaps 'twould be better if I should relent.

I like the young fellow," thought she, in a glow,
And *he* likes *me* too, for his eyes told me so."

From one thing to t'other the young maiden mused,
Of this thing and that, till she got quite confused.
" Shall I open the door ?   Yes, I will !   No, I wont !
Do I like him or not ?   Yes, I do !   No, I don't !

" Dare I open the door ? oh ! would that I could !"
She concluded at last that she could and she would.
" I'll open the door, but my best plan will be
To ascertain first their opinion of me ;
I'm doing but right—*I* was not in the plot ;
They, too, I am sure, are convinced I was not.

" I'm willing to open the door," she exclaimed,
If I do as you wish me I cannot be blamed ;
But first you must, both of you, solemnly swear
I'm your son's lawful wife—that's nothing but fair.
I as solemnly swear, if I am not his wife,
Never to go out of this room with my life."

The old folks, laughingly, gave their consent.
" We'll keep you for good, although you're but lent ;
We'll have no other daughter than you,
And our son is perfectly satisfied too.
As for *Tai-hsiao*—the bold, brazen-face !
We wouldn't allow her to enter the place."
To this, and much more, they all solemnly swore,
When *Luan-ying*, blushingly, opened the door.

We'll not relate all the young couple said,
Suffice it to say, that they went to bed,
Very much pleased with each other, no doubt:
He liked her better for shutting him out ;
She, glowing with gratitude, love, and pride,
At being thought worthy to be his bride.
Who would have thought all their plotting would bring
Such pleasure as this to the little *Luan-ying !*

The sun peeping into their chamber next morning,
  Reproachfully flashing his beams in their eyes,
Avoke the young couple ; thus giving them warning,
  As *he* had long risen, *they* too ought to rise.

At breakfast the old folks, with much kindness, met her,*
  And welcomed her there as the bride of their son :
After talking it over, they thought 'twould be better
    That none but themselves should know what had
    been done.

They had been badly treated, it must be admitted ;
  Tai-hsiao and her parents must be better taught ;
'Twould be fun for all parties to see them outwitted,
    And the schemers in turn in their own trap be
    caught.

---

* The morning after the wedding the bride is intro-
duced to the various members of the family, and, with her
husband, kowtows to those older in years than themselves ;
this is called *shuang-li*. The bride's relatives also visit
them, and spend the day there; this is called *liang-jih-chiu*.

Tai-hsiao's mother came into the room shortly after,
    And tenderly asked how *her* daughter had slept;
Luan-ying, with much blushing, and half-suppressed
    laughter,
Replied, " Very well," but her counsel she kept.

She had brought the bride's breakfast, and had no
    conception
Of what had transpired—so secure did she feel.
Each was blinding the other—her cordial reception
    Was in its way perfect, so apparently real.

She had plainly succeeded in all she had plotted;
    The first night had passed, she was satisfied now.
So contented and glad, off the old lady trotted,
    To relate her success to old *Li* and *Tai-hsiao*.

On the ninth morn the sun got up at five,
    A thing he punctually observed each day;
The same hour saw old *Li-tzu-chiu* arrive,—
    He'd come, of course, to fetch the girl away.

    But who can paint his consternation—
        His look of blank surprise and woe—
    His rueful face—his perturbation,
        When told they would not let her go!

However, there was no alternative,
    He could not take the girl away by force;
Of one great fact he now was positive—
    He *must* tell *Sun*, he saw no other course.

As he strode home he meditated,
    On this strange predicament;
First to his wife the news related,
    Then straightway off to *Sun-ssu* went.

Sun-ssu, when he heard it, grew pale with affright;
His pigtail grew stiff, 'till it stood bolt upright;
    Old *Li-tzu-chiu's* tale,
    Made him not only pale,
But turn every colour between black and white.
    He was perfectly scared,
    And with horror he stared,
When the climax was reached, as indeed well he might.

    He clawed hold of *Li,*—
    " You old villain ! " cried he,
" Give me my daughter ! I *will* have her back !
    You've stolen my daughter ! "
    " No, I haven't ! I bought her ! "
Cried *Li,* rather vexed, and in turn looking black.

" You're a beautiful father, ain't ye !
If I'd only a brush, I'd endeavour to paint ye !
Don't talk to me about *stealing* your child,
Or the chances are, you'll be getting me riled ! "

Sun's dame at this crisis appeared on the scene,
With her arms all a-kimbo, with belicose mien;
One pulled *Li* this way, the other one that,
One gave him a kick, the other a pat.
    Sun seized a chopper,
    And hit him a topper;

His wife a stone picked up,
And a great hub-bub kicked up,
While gently correcting old *Li* with the stone,
And marking his face in a style quite her own.

While the three were yelling and bawling,
Kicking and cuffing, pulling and hauling,
Up came *Liu-chên*, who had no sooner heard
The facts of the case, and what had occurred,
Than he instantly sided with old *Li-tzu-chiu*,
Which made the fight equal—two against two.
  The neighbours appearing,
  Began interfering,
Pulling *Sun* and his wife from *Li* and *Liu-chên*;
  They were no sooner parted
  Than off *Liu-chên* started
To the town, dashing off like a shot from a gun!

He rushed to the Yamên*, and hammered the drum,
Crying out, "I've been wronged, and for justice have
  come!"
The magistrate instantly opened the court;
Liu, kneeling before him, thus made his report:—

---

* In ancient times every magistrate's yamên had a drum attached to it, placed at the entrance of the justice hall; a person suffering injustice from the hands of those more powerful than himself, could beat this drum to call attention to his grievance, and the magistrate was bound to listen to his complaint. At present, although in many places the drums remain, they are seldom used.

"Your worship, my name is *Liu-chên*," he began,
"I'm a peaceful, hard-working, labouring man ;
Well, your worship, my son is betrothed to *Sun's* girl:
Sun's a poor man, like me, but a miserly churl!
For what does the heartless old vagabond do,
But *lends* the poor girl to be married to *Hu!*"
Here he stated at length this remarkable case,
His worship meanwhile getting black in the face.
"Oh! that's the way, is it, such misdeeds are done?
Bring them all up before me, I'll try every one!"
Then he threw on the ground special warrants for each,
Declaring he'd better morality teach!

The runners* to each of their houses were sent,
And like kites after carrion, off they all went.
In a short time the whole of the culprits were caught,
And into the magistrate's presence were brought.
Then, in front of his desk, they were placed in a row,
Where they knelt, and politely went through the
  kowtow.†

Said the magistrate, when this queer case he had tried,
"All tremblingly hear! This is how I decide:—
Li and *Sun*, you will each of you forty blows get,
It may teach you to look on the past with regret!
For the fault of *Tai-hsiao*, *Li* himself is to blame,—
Had she been better taught, she'd have ne'er come to
  shame.

---

  * Policemen.
  † Bumping the head on the ground.

Sun-ssu, the vile miser! craved so much for gold,
That for money his own daughter's virtue he sold.
Liu-chên, since the girl is now wedded to '*Hu,*
The money *Sun* took shall be handed to you;
'Twill add to the portion you give to your son,
And help to console him for what has been done.
Hu-lin and *Luan-ying,* you'll remain as you are;
You're wed, so I'll not your pure happiness mar.
Te-hsi, you're a scamp! and to intriguing prone;
Let your future good conduct for past faults atone;
On account of your youth I shall let you off light—
Did I punish you more 'twould be nothing but right—
Tai-hsiao, by your arts, was to wickedness led,
You'll rectify that by at once getting wed,
You're the most proper person to have *Tai-hsiao's*
    hand;
Her portion shall be the five *mu* of land.
You'll get more than you bargained for"—here he
    arose—
Five acres, a wife, and likewise—forty blows!"

The case being ended, his worship retired,
While everyone present his justice admired;
All praising the judge who could such tact display,
Discussing his merits, each went his own way.

London :
Printed by W. H. Allen & Co.,
13, Waterloo Place, Pall Mall, S.W.

.

www.ingramcontent.com/pod-product-compliance
Lightning Source LLC
Chambersburg PA
CBHW020350030726
47496CB00007B/2091